# Coots, Codgers
# and Curmudgeons

OTHER BOOKS BY HAL SISSON

The Big Bamboozle

Caverns of the Cross
*(Arsenal Pulp Press)*

# Coots, Codgers and Curmudgeons

*Things Were More Like They Used To Be Then Than They Are Now*

## Hal C. Sisson & Dwayne W. Rowe

**S**
SALAL PRESS
Victoria, BC

Copyright © 1994 Hal C. Sisson and Dwayne W. Rowe

Originally published by Orca Book Publishers, Victoria, BC

First Salal Press edition May 1999

All rights reserved. No part of this book may be reproduced in any part by any means without the written permission of the publisher, except by a reviewer who may quote brief passages in review.

**Canadian Cataloguing in Publication Data**

Sisson, Hal C., 1921-
    Coots, codgers and curmudgeons: things were more like they used to be then than they are now

1st Salal Press ed.
ISBN: 1-894012-04-6

    1. Canada, Western—Social life and customs—Humor. 2. Canadian wit and humor (English) I. Rowe, Dwayne W., 1941- II. Title

| FC3206.S57 1999 | 971.2'002'07 | C99-900492-1 |
| --- | --- | --- |
| F1060.S57 1999 | | |

Cover design by Christine Toller
Cover painting by Jack McMann

Printed and bound in Canada by
Hignell Printing Limited, Winnipeg, Manitoba

**Salal Press**
P.O. Box 36060
Victoria, BC
V9A 7J5

*To my dear wife, Roseanne, our children, Allan,
Michele, Debbie and Denise, and the grandchildren,
Tyler, Geni, Rachel, Ryan and Alex.
And for my mother, Nan Rowe, first non-aboriginal
female born in the Battle River Country – a real pioneer.*
D.W.R.

*This book is dedicated to the adage that laughter
is the clinking of a couple of unexpected coins in
the shabby pocket of life – which would be unbearable
without it. There are a great many people to whom I
could dedicate my half of this book.
Take my wife...please!*
H.C.S.

These stories are like the "oysters" we used to make in the cafes and restaurants of the towns and cities of Canada in the dirty thirties; where soda crackers, ketchup and butter were often the staples supplied at all times on each table or in each booth.

These condiments were there when you sat down to order, so you made "oysters" while waiting. With a table knife you built a very thin rim of butter along the edge of a cracker, forming a dam to hold in the ketchup you then poured into the middle. You popped the lot into your mouth and ate it like an oyster. You could get a lot of nourishment that way.

Like those oysters of yesteryear, these tales are over and gone now, faded memories slipped below the horizon of past folly, lost in the sweet embrace of remembrance; these stories are chunks of time, space and things that happen in small town Canada.

*Dwayne W. Rowe*
*Hal C. Sisson*

# Table of Contents

| | |
|---|---|
| Fist Fight for Fat Emma | 1 |
| Shangri-la | 5 |
| Running For Empties | 12 |
| Lefty Wilson and the Naked Lady | 15 |
| The Accidental Purist | 25 |
| Summer Scams | 31 |
| The Funniest Thing . . . | 39 |
| Baseball in its own Slanguage | 45 |
| Blaze of Glory | 48 |
| The Postman Cometh Twice | 54 |
| Born Again | 65 |
| An Honest to God Western Producer | 72 |
| The Luck of the Draw | 80 |
| High Prairie Hat Trick | 91 |
| Johnny | 103 |
| Double Bite | 112 |
| The Family Doc | 117 |
| Gazebos and Dreams | 125 |
| A Patient's Progress | 129 |
| A Very Public Affair | 138 |
| Bye, George – I Think You Got It | 149 |

# Fist Fight for Fat Emma

Hal C. Sisson

The kids my age in the village were all girls. Later on we got some guys, but when I was six they were all girls. We got along fine, picking flowers, playing house and stuff like that. And then a new family came to town, named Rattee. Their youngest son was my age — I can't remember now if Billie was a week older or a week younger than I — it doesn't matter. Anyway, being the only two boys, we started to play together right off.

"Let's go picking flowers," I said that first day. The prairie was loaded with wildflowers in those days when there was a lot of prairie left.

"Naw, let's go killing gophers," replied Billie. I went with him, but I didn't like killing gophers much. Not at first anyway. But then I guess you can get used to anything. The gophers never seemed to, though.

Every once in a while I tried to revert to my former sissified mode of play and balked at doing what he wanted. Billie would then pick a fight and beat on me instead of the local wildlife. He wasn't vicious, but you got scratched and dirtied up a lot. To these unwarranted attacks I never put up much resistance. Billie liked fighting. I didn't and he knew it. I'd go home crying to my mother and she'd comfort me.

With his father owning the only store in the village like he did, it always seemed a simple thing for Billie to get his hands on a couple of chocolate bars. They were only a nickel in the Dirty Thirties, remember. My favourite was one called Fat Emma, a delicious foamy marshmallow dipped in dark chocolate. After a scrap, Billie would always give me one and we'd be friends again. And before long we'd be playing cowboys and Indians together. He'd be the cowboys and pretty soon the plot would call for them to beat up on the Indians, which was me.

Well, my dad soon found out about this scenario — from my mother, I guess, or maybe I came home bawling one time, expecting some milk and sympathy, and he happened to be around the house. Dad took me aside and explained the facts of life to me.

"If you come home one more time, beat-up and bawling, and saying that Billie Rattee cleaned your clock," he said, "then I am informing you here and now, young man, that the licking you are going to get from me will make your go-rounds with little Billie feel like a Sunday school picnic. Now get your butt down there and don't come back until you've given him a licking."

I looked up at my father, a guy I really liked, even though he could be a disciplinarian at times. I can still remember the expression on his face. I knew from that look that he was mad and deadly serious. I was frightened as I went down the street to the only crossroads in town, turned the corner and headed for the general store. I knocked on the side door to the residence behind the store. Billie's mother was always nice to me. When she answered the door, I asked her if Billie could come out and play. He could and he did. I noticed that he had two fat Emmas in his shirt pocket.

There was a high board fence around the Rattees' yard. About halfway down one side was a spot where one board was missing and I motioned to Billie to follow me through the opening.

"I've got something real good to show you, Billie," I said.

I was still real scared. I wondered if he could see me shaking, as we went into the old weedy vacant lot on the other side of the fence — the place had begun to look to me like a Roman amphitheatre. This was no flower picking expedition with little Sally Neff.

I turned to face Billie just as he reached into his pocket for the chocolate bars. For a moment I hesitated. Why didn't I just take that delicious piece of confection and forget about the Christians and the lions bit? I could taste the lovely soft marshmallow and the sweet chocolate — but I could also see my father's face and remember his words.

I let Billie have it in the chops with all the force I could muster. I figured that's what he'd do, get the first punch in. Anyway, this was no time for Marquess of Queensberry rules — too much was at stake. I leapt on top of him as he stumbled backward, bearing him to the ground. In my excited state my arms were flailing like windmills, so that even though there was little sense of direction, I was getting in a lot of blows. It was then and there that I learned the value of the first-strike-sneaky-surprise attack. That and the sheer inner excitement and necessity of emerging the victor won the day. I wasn't going back to my dad to get the tanning he had promised; I was going back to get some praise.

Poor Billie never stood a chance. I think he was as dumbfounded at the suddenness of the onslaught as at its ferocity. He fought for a while, but he was down and he was getting pummeled. This was a new experience for him and he pretty quickly yelled uncle.

That was our last fight and I whomped him good, even though he had won the first half dozen. The spoils of war were not something I knew much about at the time, but victory deserves its reward. I ripped the two Fat Emmas out of Billie's pocket and took off on the run, back through the fence, down the street and home.

The bars were a little squashed but I gave one to my dad. He looked at it, at my dirt-covered clothes, smiled and thanked me for the Fat Emma.

Billie Rattee was my best friend from that day on. He remained my best friend until we were both twenty-two and he got killed flying a Spitfire out of Malta in WWII. He wasn't exactly fighting at the time, he was on the ground, a victim of faulty traffic control and another allied plane.

Billie, how come you forgot to watch out for sudden danger when you least expected it? And from your friends yet? I thought I had taught you about that. You never got to be an air ace, but you didn't have to worry about getting old either. I wish they still made Fat Emma bars. I owe you two.

# Shangri-la

Dwayne W. Rowe

I grew up in Northern Alberta, during the forties and fifties, thinking Velveeta was cheese. My uncles, having borrowed a recipe from my Swedish grandfather without bothering to have him translate it into English, used it to create a concoction of pickled herring and lutefisk intended as a cure for the constant stomach troubles we got from drinking alkali water from our well. Nobody north of Dixonville had any decent drinking water and dowsers had been hired, fired and beaten for their failures.

Dr. Fowler's Extract of Wild Strawberry was a big seller in the general store. One fellow had been keeping company with a young lady for several years and each time she came down with a bout of diarrhea he would send her over some Dr. Fowler's. Their relationship came to an end, but her intestinal disorder did not. One afternoon the erstwhile lovers met on the street and she said, plaintively, "You don't send me Fowler's anymore!" This, you must remember, took place long ago while Barbra Streisand's nose was still forming.

The Mackenzie Highway ran right through the middle of town. In fact, it was the middle of town, doubling as Main Street. Huge semi-trailer outfits would come barrelling down the hill, past the imaginary dividing line that turned The Highway into Main Street, coasting downwards, faster and faster, over the bridge, engines popping, until they hit the hill on the other side, gearing down and snorting up the slope that had again become The Highway.

In the summer the dust would hang for hours. In order to cross from the drugstore to the pool hall on the other side of Main Street, one cocked an ear towards the downhill, and hearing nothing, ran like hell to get across. Every summer somebody would get clobbered in the middle of the dust cloud by some guy coasting into town in his old pickup, out of gas, trying to make it to Black Mike's service station near the bridge. In fact, at the height of one drought, during a busy trucking season, you couldn't reach the other side of main street; you had to be born there.

Down by the bridge, across from Black Mike's, was the Post Office. For some reason U-turns were permitted and people would drive down the hill into town, peering through the dust, then, glimpsing the bridge, would realize they had missed the turn-off to the Post Office. So, they would make a U-turn and proceed up the gravelled street looking for some storefront that looked familiar. Meanwhile, the big semis would come racing down the street and the locals would be running back and forth through the dust, zig-zagging like chickens, for the same reason as the chickens, to get to the other side. Once across, as Gertrude Stein observed about Oakland, California, there was no there there. Except Brown's Style Shop, the Pool Hall, Sam Fong's Cafe and Johnny's Barber Shoppe.

In the pool hall, games of pea pool, snooker, Boston and Russian billiards were occupying the eight tables. Women were absolutely forbidden to enter. Underage kids hung around the doorway hoping to be sent by some woman as a messenger to page a husband, boyfriend or father to come outside and receive some news about business or family matters. It was a classic win-win situation, although we didn't know that terminology back then. The women didn't have to go into that foul-smelling dungeon; the men had their haven; the underage geeks could gain entry, however fleeting, into the sanctum sanctorum, the Valhalla of their non-masturbatory dreams; and nobody ever had to look as though they were hen-pecked or at the beck and call of some woman.

All chewing-out and shin-kicking took place in private, on the sidewalk, just at the edge of the dust. Most of the wives had the decency not to let loose with any loud language until a semi would roar by and then she'd kick her man or give him a really good whack as the dust roiled up and washed against the pool hall like a tidal wave, blotting out the few clear patches between the fly specks on the windows. None of the men inside ever deliberately gawked out in these kinds of situations, but now and then somebody would peek out to see if the mail truck had come in yet.

When the fellow outside had finished receiving his news, he would come back into the pool hall, mosey over to the table, pick up the cue and with a real "thock," drive the cue ball onto his target. A couple of shots later, when it was his turn to shoot he'd say to nobody, "Neighbour told the wife it looks like rain — better get goin' before that goddamn hill gets any wetter. Thanks for the game."

One time, Charlie Nipshank, who wasn't supposed to be doing any drinking or playing pool, had done one and was doing the other, when his wife Edna sent in a boy with a message to call Charlie out. She got hold of him right there on the sidewalk and in the words of Rollie C., who got to the only clear spot in the window, Edna "kicked the living shit out of him." When Charlie came back into the pool hall, looking like he'd tangled with a semi, he walked over to the pop machine, pulled out a Coke and drained it in one gulp.

Putting the empty back in the wire rack he said, "Edna tells me there's a sale on binder twine up at the Co-op."

"Shit," said a couple of guys, slapping their palms to

their foreheads, and they ran out of the pool hall straight up to the Co-op where, discovering no bargains to be had, went ahead and paid regular price for a couple of rolls.

Notwithstanding the proximity of Johnny's Barber Shoppe, the pool hall itself had a chair. The proprietor doubled as a barber and he would leave in the middle of a trim to go rack the balls. On a busy day he'd rack a little, trim a little, rack some more and collect money for the tables. A haircut could take a couple of hours. Sometimes when a table would come open, the person getting the trim would leap out of the chair, hand the apron to a new customer and shoot a game or two. Then, during a lull, either that day or within a week or so, Neil, the barber-proprietor, would finish off the haircut.

One day, Archie Daigle, who was mostly bald, came in for a trim and Bill Brown, who was racking the snooker balls, said, "Neil, you should only charge him half-price for a haircut *(pause)* . . . but you can double the cost of a shave *(pause)* . . . 'cause his face is twic't as long." If you were shooting pool with Bill and his cue ball was meandering around the table, about to scratch in a pocket, he would thump the base of his cue on the floor and holler, "Don't go down in the mines today — there's plenty of coal on top." His favourite joke was: One feller says t'other feller, "Are the squirrels very thick around here?" And the first feller says, "Oh, about as thick as your wrist." That was it for Bill's reservoir of jokes, but it did have a certain Woody Allen cast to it. Maybe Bill was ahead of his time, because he wasn't much with it in those days.

Some of the boys used to get together for a game of cards from time to time. The favourite local game was called stook, basically a doltish version of Blackjack or 21. No one ever figured out that the player with the biggest bankroll would inevitably win because all he had to do was wait for an ace or face card and then match the pot. The players would gather after the stores closed at 10:00 PM Saturday night and the game would start.

The local Chinese cafe changed hands seven times in ten years over the stook table. Sunday morning the former owner would be the dishwasher and then a few months later would be the owner again and there would be a new dishwasher. Nobody ever said, "Heard you lost your cafe." Then again, nobody ever said, "Heard you won your cafe back."

Sometimes the intelligentsia played a game called Smear, which was a combination of bridge and whist that involved bidding and taking tricks. If you bid and didn't make it, you had to take a "hickey." And if you bid and made the whole damn thing that was "mooning." This is not to be confused with the later vulgar practice of baring one's backside in public, although if a person bid for a moon and didn't make it there was always the potential of losing your ass.

There were times when the card games were too slow and so a dozen or so of the guys would sit around the back of the barber shop and match coins, heads or tails. They would match for cars, stoves, guns, dogs and pieces of farm equipment. Come seeding time an unlucky player would have to borrow a seed drill from his neighbour, which set back his seeding time until the owner was finished. With my own eyes I have seen two guys flip coins for a disk against a portable grain auger. Then the auger and disk were lost when wagered for a pickup truck and on it went. Nobody ever bothered to register a change in the ownership because, as likely as not, there was never any change in the physical possession of the item. Except for the seed drills.

Saturday night was incredible. The population of the town, normally about six hundred, swelled to double. One farmer who had about twelve kids would haul them into town in the back of his grain truck and their heads would project over the box in descending order of height and seniority until you couldn't see any more heads. But, you knew another half-dozen kids were inside because you could see their little white knuckles hanging on to the edge of the top of the box.

The local theatre had two shows, one at 7:00 PM and the

other at 9:00. On Saturday nights all of the shows were Westerns and one of the favourites was anything with "One-eyed Ronnie Reagan," who was so named because he was always squinting. In those days it was pronounced, Ree-gun. Randolph Scott and Rod Cameron from Calgary were well-liked as were Jimmy Stewart and the Duke.

Now and then a Catholic film like "Going My Way" would be showing and there wouldn't be three Protestants in the crowd. The theatre owner, who growled instead of talking, would catch hell from the non-Catholics.

"Hope the Missus and me don't have to quit comin' to the show. Maybe you'd best think about not gettin' too many of them Dogan films."

"Aarggh, ach, hhrrh, lacchhh," the owner would reply, and the complainant would wander off, secure in the belief that One-Eyed Ronnie Ree-gun would soon ride again.

When *Gone With the Wind* first played nobody had ever seen a show that had an intermission, so while Atlanta was still burning, about ninety percent of the crowd went home. Next day in Fong's Cafe they remarked over coffee, "Hellava show ... good fire ... but the ending is the shits!" The theatre owner had a couple of kids who could talk instead of growl, so they ran around town and spread the word and most of the opening night patrons went back the next night and saw the rest of the show. Then in Fong's Cafe the comments went like this: "That Clark Gable is kind of a pretty boy, but he ain't no sissy ... that uppity O'Hara gal got what she deserved."

One time the film distributor really screwed up and decided to send a little culture our way by shipping, on the bus, that classic, *Les Misérables*. In those days the theatres displayed those grand movie posters. A local fellow, peering at the poster, was obviously perplexed and yelled across the street to his friend, "Who in hell is this guy Les Miserables?" The sidekick pondered for a moment and declared proudly, "Les, why hell, he's the new hired hand over at the Gummesons."

Saturday night was the best of all. It was magic. Once the crowds had cleared out of the stores, the street and the bar, then, likely as not, a breeze would blow down Main Street and clear away the dust. When it did, the moon would come out, all big and ripe, and shine off the water tank on top of the hill overlooking town and you could make out the red lettering painted on the side of the silver tank: Welcome to Manning: The Shangri-La of the North.

# Running For Empties

Hal C. Sisson

At the age of seven I had never heard of the cliché "rich beyond your wildest dreams," or I would have used it. But I did get an immediate feeling of affluence when I spotted the jackpot on the slope of a wide gully leading into the left side of that dirt country road. Glass glinted in the sun for several moments and then we were past, with me yelling to my father to stop the car, which he did about a hundred yards down the road. I piled out of the passenger side onto the grass verge, ran through the shallow ditch to the three strand barbed-wire fence, gingered my way through it, and raced down the pasture back toward the gully on whose grassy side I had gotten the quick glimpse of the dark green and brown bonanza of bottles. Breaking over the brow, I started down the slope of the ravine, running toward the largest bunch of beer bottles I had ever found.

Two-bits a dozen they were in those days — two cents each and I guessed they just threw in the extra penny because they were such nice guys down at the Beer Bottle

Exchange Depot on Manitoba Street. Because my father taught grades one to ten in a one-room schoolhouse in Pasqua, nine miles from Moose Jaw, the car — some kind of Ford with black canvas top and side curtains — was a necessity; and from the vantage of the co-pilot's seat I had become an expert observer by the age of six. I could spot a beer bottle in a Saskatchewan ditch whose presence would evade an optometrist. It probably cost my father more to stop and start the car than I ever made in my avid search for wealth, courtesy of the many drinking drivers and their passengers who threw this treasure into the ditches and fields as they cruised the highways and back roads of the prairies. Many years later that was still the custom. Maybe it still is, although roads are now much wider, cars travel much too fast, and there are littering laws and many, many more cop cars on the road. Furthermore, nowadays you can get a legal drink anywhere, and not just at the few and far between, all male, beer parlours of the twenties and thirties.

Now a lost art, the throw of the empty in those days had been perfected. Grasping the bottle by the long neck, you stuck your arm out the side of the car and looped it up and over the roof of the vehicle as far as you could, into the opposite ditch or field. Very fastidious really — it was not considered good form to have the bottle smash on the gravel roads — after all, flat tires were already too regular a feature of motoring to add to the likelihood of more repeated occurrence. The idea was to create a soft landing in the weed- and water-filled ditches in the summer or the snow in the winter.

The spring was the best time to collect beer bottles. As the snow melted, the bottles magically appeared from their winter hiding places, to be gleaned by aficionados such as myself. Too easy. What I really liked was the challenge of spotting their presence in the summer's abundant grass.

They came in ones, sometimes twos and threes over a short stretch, and occasionally you'd find a whole case of empties. However, you never found hundreds and hundreds of them in one spot — well, except at the bottle exchange, where they were stacked in cases by the thousands, waiting to go back to the brewery for a refill.

So this was it, in a side gully off a country road near my grandfather's farm near Crestwind, the biggest find of my career, the one that would make me financially independent. I tried to pick one up — it was broken. I searched frantically, but carefully, around and about the foot-deep mound of glass. I ran around the fringes. I looked at the scattered pieces. And I burst into tears. Desolation! Every last one of those beer bottles was broken. A moment of fool-begged time I remember — life is a dream from which you frequently are awakened by reality.

My dad soon arrived on the scene and consoled me, pointing out some other debris, some gouges in the gullyside, a broken fence, which indicated that a beer truck must have rolled to its demise at this location.

That's life, I guess...or death! I had $48.75 in my beer bottle bank account at the time my dad died of streptococcal blood poisoning a couple of years later, five or six years before they discovered the sulfanilamide drug and its derivatives. We sold the car, moved to town, I drew the goddamn money from the bank and gave it to my mother to help with the groceries. My dad was thirty, hadn't ever been sick, just starting out, really. He cut his finger on a broken beer bottle.

# Lefty Wilson and the Naked Lady

Hal C. Sisson

Her skin had a sort of opalescence, which in certain lighting became a chameleon milky iridescence. It was as if she had more than one layer covering her pure, snowy, imperfectly transparent body. Love for the Naked Lady still shone in my heart like a dream. I had never wanted to lose her — but I did. A long time ago. In a contest of skill, to be sure, but gambled away nevertheless.

Haphazard fortune sometimes gives a second chance, and this very afternoon, window shopping along Royale Street, suddenly there she was, and I had a gut feeling I could possess her again. Oh, the cost would be more than what I'd paid way back then. I knew that, but I could now afford whatever was asked. How much could it be? No matter, I wanted her again, at any price.

She lay there, naked as usual, in the window of the old shop, and I walked through the door to talk about price.

"How much is she, you ask?" said the Madame. "Fifty dollars."

"Fifty dollars!" I repeated. Pause for thought.

The thirties were a long time ago, but has inflation upped the price of anything one hundred times? Well, what else is new.

The raddled old harridan took my money. The naked lady was to be mine once more. The best milkie I'd ever seen, like a moonstone, identical to the one I had owned those many years ago.

Could it be the same one? Holding the marble up to the sunlight in the street, I thought of Lefty Wilson and Rose Mitchell for the first time in many years. They were both closely linked in my mind to this marvelous three-quarter inch marble, my best shooter, for use only in the closest of games. Rose had been as pretty as the aggie I had named the Naked Lady; and Lefty was my main and worthy opponent when we played for keeps on the Christopher Public School grounds a long time ago in the hometown of my boyhood days. We had played marbles for both Rose and the Naked Lady.

## Lefty

Grade eight is about the limit of your marble playing days. You played in the spring. Almost before the first robin started hopping on the lawn, out came the marbles. Then, a few weeks later, almost as suddenly as they had appeared, the marbles were gone. Most everyone played, and most everyone gambled their marbles, but by grade eight, Lefty Wilson and I were the two players most feared on the school playground. We were never friends per se, always seeming to travel in the different little groups that keep forming and reforming in public school. Except at marble time — then we were friendly rivals who met often.

I spoke of a lawn, of which we had very little at Christopher. What we did have was a level gravel pit with some very hardy weeds around the edges, surrounded by a caragana hedge and a line of bedraggled trees on the boulevard.

On this surface the serious marble players would kick out all the rocks and stones, then scuff the dirt surface as smooth, flat and hard as possible, and draw a ring. Serious poker players won't play outlandish card games with wild cards, like Midnight Baseball or Piss in the Ocean, only playing Draw or Stud. So we too no longer played what we considered dumb juvenile marble games like Chasies, Holy Bang, Funsies or Bung-hole. We would on occasion play Poison Ring, Black Snake or Killer, which were games for the best of shooters. The most popular was the real national rules game called Ringer. You had to shoot with ease and deadly accuracy to do well in that game. Otherwise you lost all your marbles.

Ringer was played in a ten-foot-diameter circle with each player placing an equal number of marbles in the centre of the ring in the form of a cross. Knock a marble out and it was yours. You set your own rules when you played for keeps, and usually you had to knuckle a certain number out while shooting from the edge of the ring, before you could dribble in amongst the remaining dibs. That position could be dangerous because if another player knocked out your shooter you were out of the game. Well, you probably all know the rules anyway.

The players inspected the agates that were being wagered to be sure they were playing for approximate equal value. Nobody wanted to put up a spotless lemonade corkscrew against a chipped swirl. The kids had an unwritten code of marble values.

## The Girl

Rose always reminded me of my favourite shooter, the Naked Lady. My marble didn't, of course, have bodily functions, and at first I could not think that Rose had either. Later on, my fevered brain imagined that she might have, and I have to admit that I kept trying to find out. (After all, if an Egyptian asp is a snake in the grass, why is a grasp in the ass a goose?) This was the bewitching girl who threatened my eventual failed friendship with Lefty Wilson, the second-best (my opinion, not his) marble shooter in town.

## The Marbles

The names probably change with the years. Marbles aren't played as much as they used to be, before TV and all the modern distractions. But often what kids called marbles made more sense than the names the makers gave them. Names such as snakes and 7 Up's, bumble-bees, the cub scout, the black widow or wasp. There were blue moons and foggies, and a gassie that looked like a puddle of water with gasoline in it.

## The School

As I said, it was essentially a rockpile surrounded by a low, spiked, wrought-iron fence and a ragged caragana hedge. A building of standard beige brick, standing in the middle of a city block, built to house any given number of students. The two sides and back were divided into boys' and girls' playgrounds. These were fenced off from the strip directly in front of the school, which sported a cement sidewalk and the only grass, with flowered borders, leading to a fancy front entrance which no one was ever seen to use. There were no school laws that we knew of, no Magna Carta as it were — no law west of the Pecos — just a form of frontier justice, administered by the head honchos.

    The teachers all had their idiosyncrasies. Don Harris, the vice-principal, taught grade seven. A good enough guy when not in a temper, he played piano on the side in area dance halls. Didn't find that out till I was a little older and attended a dance at the Odd Fellows Hall (locally called the "Bucket of Blood" or if you'd rather, the "Gonorrhea Racetrack"). He had one gimpy leg, shorter than the other, and probably the result of polio, or a birth defect. No one dared ask. I can't remember the kid's name — the kid at whom

Harris got so violently mad one June afternoon — but no one who saw it can ever forget Harris the Teacher chasing this slightly tubby student around and around the classroom, trying to get close enough to kick the kid in the ass. This daily sacrificial lamb wouldn't go to the cloakroom to get the strap, and this maddened the vice-principal. Harris would gain sufficient ground to execute a drop kick at his victim's butt — but the gimpy leg would then come into play, slowing him down and putting him off stride just enough that his kicking foot would barely miss. He was literally a one-legged man in an ass-kicking contest. This went on till they were both exhausted. Whoever laughed was going to get it next, we knew, so this charade went on in almost complete silence. One of the best races I have seen to this day.

The grade seven room was on the ground floor in one corner of the school; it therefore had windows on two sides overlooking the boys' playground. On a hot June afternoon near the end of term, all the windows would be opened as wide as possible. We used fountain pens in those days, which required the use of ink and ink bottles. Don instructed all students whose ink bottles became empty to deposit same on his desk, complete with tops. As we laboured over some work assignment in whatever, Don hippity hopped along the windowed sides of the classroom, keeping the playground under surveillance for stray dogs. He carried several ink bottles on his person, hoping for a good shot. Sometimes he'd whistle to get their attention — so that the dogs would stop momentarily and present a stationary target. A great number of canines — those sons of bitches in Harris's terminology — loping across the grounds, did not know that they had now entered the OK Corral and were about to meet the most accurate and fastest ink bottle in the west. We'd try to get a quick look when he fired off a bottle, but you could tell if Harris scored a hit, because loud yelping ensued. If successful, we knew enough to cheer. Some refrained, usually the girls, as it was a form of cruelty to animals, not to speak of the amount of broken glass spread over a wide area of playground. Nobody ever slid into third or home base in the softball games, even if it might mean a run to be scored against a rival school. Not on that rock and glass pile. Encourage the other team to steal bases —you stood a chance of getting rid of those of their players who fancied themselves in that role.

The principal was Wm. A. Kirkpatrick, affectionately known as "Sir" —a middle-aged, balding, lecherous pervert, whom even Clarence Thomas would convict of sexual harassment. His favourite pastime was to catch some nubile and budding young grade eight female in some academic error. Whereupon he would have her up to the front of the class to undergo an inquisition as to her knowledge of the subject matter. The girls would be so frightened, of course, that they usually forgot what they did know. In which case Wm. A. used a ruler or pointer, and at each incorrect response, he would jab his weapon just above the armpit in the crease of the shoulder. From there he would quickly move inward until he was actually jabbing them in the boobs, while stating emphatically, "You're a Dub! You're a Dub!" This seemed to arouse his libido, as evidenced by the increased tightness of his pants. It wasn't school the girls disliked but the principal of the thing.

## The Gamble

Lefty and I had pretty well cleaned out the other shooters at Christopher. We'd gone to the marble tournaments at other locales and won. As expert shooters, we had foraged afar to other city schools and neighbourhoods looking for action, almost invariably playing for keeps with marble slingers we might seldom see again. We had our off days but we usually won multi mibs and clodknockers. I remember winning a china-blue onion-skin shooter with loads of mica, and Lefty once won a patched, opaque comic-character marble with Betty Boop imprinted in the surface. The time was late grade eight and the marble season was ending.

So who was there left to play? It became obvious. We were going to have to play each other. A Shoot Out! Now, in playing Ringer with only two players, if you "killed" your opponent's shooter, you were the only player left and, therefore, as the other kid was out of the game, you got all the marbles left in the ring. A new game was started with the agreed ante of ducks or clams again placed in the ring by each player. I made the first proposal. We would each choose our twenty-five best marbles and play Ringer till one of us won them all.

I had forgotten how much Lefty wanted both Rose Mitchell and the Naked Lady. Neither of us had any proprietary rights to Rose, but I did own the shooter which he highly prized and coveted.

Naturally, the winner would keep all the target miggs, but Lefty suggested that whoever won got a clear field with Mitchell, and the other guy had to promise that he would back off from any attempt to get friendlier with Rose. That was Jim Dandy by me, but then Lefty came up with the catch. He would only agree to play if the loser got the other guy's shooter; in my case, the Naked Lady no less. Lefty was shooting with an excellent rainbow reeler, a real marble marble, a realie.

There was a subconscious streak of pragmatism in me, even in those youthful days. I figured the odds. We were evenly matched as to skill, so they were fifty-fifty in that respect. If I won I got two things, a clearer field with Rose and what amounted to the unofficial Marble Championship of the City. And I could only lose one thing — the Naked Lady. Two reasons for, one against — two to one odds in my favour. I took the gamble.

So, who really won? I've pondered that on occasion. The game raged back and forth on the best ring in the school yard, and as they say in the St. James Infirmary Blues, "a goodly crowd was there." We started right after the four o'clock bell and played until it was nearly too dark to see.

As each individual game in the contest was played, I gradually gained the upper hand until Lefty had his last five marbles in the ring. I always played well when my shooter was the Naked Lady.

Good marbles is much like shooting good pool. How you hit the object marble dictates where your shooter is going to come to rest. Just as in snooker, "English" can be obtained; in marbles the thumb acts in the same manner as the cue tip — under the marble for backspin, toward the top for topspin. Strategy calls for not leaving your shooter in the ring if you fail to knock out one of the dibs. If you stun the target marble, it goes out and your shooter stays very near the point of impact, ready to take your next shot at another nearby marble. The closer you stay to the marbles left in the ring, the more you clean up. But at times you want to strike the object marble with side in order to get your shooter to carom to another part of the ring. But sometimes and for some reason, the dib does not quite depart the ring, and worse still, your shooter stays in the ring also, sometimes uncomfortably close to the edge. It is now no longer your shot as you haven't made a dib, you can't run for cover by purposely shooting out, and you are at the mercy of your opponent. Ten feet is a long distance to accurately knuckle a small marble, but good players are extremely accurate — and when you cut this distance down to one or two feet, someone is likely to go down the tubes.

On my first shot of the last game, I hit two mibs, my shooter and one marble exiting the ring, but leaving a snooger, which is a 'commie rat' target marble, near the rim of the ring. It was a good set-up for my next shot but I made a "mistook" — I called "slips." But the Naked Lady had traveled far more than ten inches and therefore had to be considered a shot. I was now left vulnerable in the ring; Lefty yelled "fan, everies" and circled the playing ring, seeking his best playing position. He knuckled down, preparing to ride the snooger by hitting it a glancing blow, knocking it from the ring, while bouncing his shooter into the mass of easy target marbles and my shooter in the centre. I was as good as dead in the dirt in this game.

Marbles do many different things. The snooger didn't have to move very far to go out of the ring; so Lefty aimed too soft a shot at the right side of the snooger — a near miss and his shooter spun madly in some loose dirt, slowing its progress until it came to rest within easy range of the Naked Lady.

And that's what happened to Lefty. I "killed" him and won the Shoot Out. It was the last game of marbles I ever played. The marble season was over for all time. I had won using the Naked Lady which is why I lost her. She never wanted me to lose, and I realized later that her use had added to my concentration, which is really the thing that makes any pool shark or marble player successful.

I gave him the Naked Lady, what else could I do. Did Lefty keep his part of the bargain? I'm not sure, but you do learn a lot of things about life as you grow older. Sometime later, after the big game, I bought a box of chocolates and went over to the apartment where Rose lived. She answered the door. I proffered the chocolates, which she took with gracious thanks, but she did not invite me in. She could see my surprise, but she explained that she had company and could we get together again soon. Yeah, well sure, I could take a rain check.

School was out, so I didn't see Lefty around for a few days. He never said he'd been there, but he kept talking about how much he liked chocolates, especially Black Magic ones. We didn't swear much in those days, but if Lefty had been partaking of my gift of chocolates to Rose, then cheese on crackers got all muddy, he was a rectal hiccup and no friend of mine. As it happened he moved out of town shortly thereafter. I heard many years later that he now lives in the Maritimes.

I kept dating Rose sporadically, never getting to first base, let alone sliding home in a bunch of broken ink bottles. Whenever I'd call I would meet her mother. Good looking woman, Mrs. Mitchell, always immaculately coiffed and dressed. No man around, widowed or more likely divorced, I don't remember. She always appeared as if she was amused at something or other. Likely at the continual parade of boys and young men who traipsed into their home after Rose. Now Mrs. Mitchell had a great product there, but what I didn't know, or failed to realize at the time, was that she was into marketing. She was training Rose for bigger and better things, as all mothers do, but often with little result or cooperation.

Some allegedly lucky guy eventually got Rose, or so I heard. Someone a lot richer and fatter than I, and 4F to boot. And that's the way the marbles roll. Did Mrs. Mitchell's gambit pay off in spades for Rose — and is Rose sharing her chocolates with whomsoever she wishes? I don't care!

Am I the winner?

Well now, I was Marble Champ in 1935; but I don't have all my marbles anymore. Neither Lefty nor I got Rose, so that all evened out. However, I am now holding the Naked Lady and this time it's for keeps!

# The Accidental Purist
Dwayne W. Rowe

On any farm, even little bitty two-acre ones, kids are an accident looking to happen. Apart from the potential for accidents in the pure and ordinary sense, there is a lot of foolishness going on, which, if it turns bad and it usually does, can cause problems.

With me it wasn't only on the farm that bad things happened, but a fair amount of trouble did find me there.

My grandfather always used a fork to undo a really tight knot in his shoelace. He would bend over the shoe with a fork, insert one of the tines into the lace just under the knot and worry it back and forth and then lift up the fork and, voilà, the knot would be undone. I must have watched this a dozen times.

One day, when I couldn't undo my shoelace, I went into the kitchen and got a fork. As I had seen Grandad Nord do again and again, I inserted the tine into the knot and pulled upwards. The knot came undone like it was supposed to. But unfortunately, the fork kept on coming up in an arc until it imbedded itself in the meaty part of my nose just where the bridge becomes the tip. All four tines punctured my nose. The blood shot out like four little artesian wells. It wasn't so bad if I held my fingers over the holes but it was like playing a flute and every time I lifted one finger or the other a fount of blood would spurt up. I managed to get the bleeding stopped by plugging the holes with axle grease and wore a Band-Aid until it healed up, blaming the whole business on sunburn.

My parents had, of course, forbidden me to play with knives. A couple of years went by and then, on my twelfth birthday, Grandad thought I was old enough to be responsible for handling sharp instruments. He gave me a Swedish army knife that had a massive main blade held in place by a powerful spring. I opened it up, looked at it and then tried to close the blade gently, but it suddenly let go and came down like a guillotine on the webbing between the thumb and the forefinger of my hand. The thumb drooped away from the muscle holding it and, although it eventually grew back more or less the way it was intended, word leaked out and my parents confiscated the knife. To this day I haven't gotten it back.

I had a great bicycle which my Dad bought for me at the Co-op store in North Star. It had balloon tires, whitewalls, and we installed a headlight, speedometer and a basket made of steel which could hold hundreds of pounds of stuff. It was the Cadillac of bikes. It didn't have much low-end power, but, once it was rolling, the speed could be maintained with little effort.

One bright summer day I was pedalling down the main (and only) street in North Star. I was cruising comfortably along the edge of the gravel road when I decided to change lanes to the middle where the rocks were a little smaller. There was, of course, no traffic to speak of in those days. Just the same I did the proper over-the-shoulder check as I'd been taught. When I turned around to face the front again, I ran smack into the back of a parked grain truck. I hit the box of the truck with such force that it drove my lower teeth through my upper lip and vice-versa. I was just a little bit stunned by all of this. In fact, I couldn't figure out what in hell had happened. It took me a few minutes to straighten out the bike so it was rideable.

Then I headed out to the farm and tried to explain to my uncles, George and Oscar, what had happened. But they had trouble understanding me because of the teeth sticking through the lip.

"I thwit uh thwuck," I told them, "a thwuck bock wif my faith." They looked at those little white tips of teeth poking out through the skin and started to laugh and slap their overalls. Once they settled down they were able to pry the skin over the teeth and to clean me up a bit before my parents came home.

For weeks afterwards my face was flat and, when I drank Kool-Aid, it would leak out through the holes. Had I done the hole-in-the-nose trick at the same time, I would have had a face like a lawn-soaker hose. Unfortunately, all of this happened about the time of the incident with the Swedish knife. If my thumb would have stood up on its own, I would have used it to hitch a ride out of town.

One time about six of us kids were taking turns jumping up and down on a plank which was straddled over two big logs. The plank was quite springy and I moved close to the jumpers to inform them it was my turn and stuck my foot under the plank which was bending down to the ground before springing back. Unbeknownst to me, there was a spike protruding through the middle of the plank and, as the boys jumped up and down, the plank bent back and forth and drove the spike through my foot on a repeated basis much as a sewing machine needle in the hands of an artisan goes through fabric.

By the time I realized what had transpired, or was able to do anything about it, my foot had six holes in it. It later became infected from the rust and dirt on the spike. I limped around for weeks wondering what other parts of my body I could conceivably puncture before the summer was out. I didn't have long to wait.

A few days after my foot healed, a gang of us were out in the field playing football. Ever the enthusiast, I rushed the kicker. The ball came off the end of his foot at about two hundred miles an hour and the pointy end hit me square between the eyes. I had been wearing wire-framed glasses since the age of six and the force of the impact not only bent the frames into a modern-art form, it squished the nosepieces into the bridge of my nose. The force of the blow was such that I couldn't dig deep enough into the flesh to pry them loose. So I ended up riding my bike to Dr. Dwan's office. There I had to sit in the waiting room for an hour or so until he could see me. It is bad enough having to read a three-year-old *Life* magazine without the burden of twisting your head around to conform with the way your glasses have become attached to your face.

I should have been charging amusement tax in those days. Dr. Dwan not only nearly killed himself laughing at my nose, but, before he began to surgically extricate the remains of the spectacles from inside my face, he called in his nurse to corroborate my humiliation.

My dumbest accident happened in town during a cold snap in January of 1955. It was at least fifty below and I was curling lead on my dad's rink. I was late for the seven o'clock draw and was running like the wind. I wore moccasins in those days and, even with insoles, you couldn't let your feet contact the ground for longer than a nano-second in that kind of weather. I decided to take a short cut through an alley and across a gravel pit which was being used as a pad for a couple of mobile homes. I came barrelling downhill, mouth wide open, sucking in great gobs of frozen air to fuel my lungs for the tremendous power needed to maintain my pace, when I ran into a clothesline.

There never has been a more apt expression in the English language than to say someone was "clotheslined." The feet keep going but the upper body stops. I was lying on my back in the snow wondering what in hell had now come to pass in my miserable life, when I noticed a whitish object lying on top of my mitt. On inspection it turned out to be a tooth, complete with root. I soon discovered it to have been a back molar, which a few seconds before had been in my mouth. Obviously, the clothesline had caught me square across the mouth, hooked under the molar at the gum line and, when I fell, hawked it out as neat as one could ever want. Because of the cold there was little or no bleeding, so I put the tooth in the pocket of my parka and ran down to the curling rink.

When I went onto the ice, Dad could see that my mouth had been torn, more or less ear-to-ear, though at first I could tell he thought I was grinning about something. Dr. Dwan, who played the third on our team, decided stitches weren't required, probably because I had been so late; we were about to forfeit the end, and a loss at that point in the schedule could have affected our drive for the club championship. So, until the marks on my face healed up, I looked like a golfball that had been hit by some duffer with a nine-iron. I didn't appreciate being called Smiley. Tooth transplanting had never been heard of in those gentler times and to this day I have to pluck food out of that great, gaping cavern in the back of my mouth — a constant reminder of another childhood disaster.

As an adult I talked to my uncle George about an incident that happened when I wasn't much more than about three years old. I was running around the bottom of the garage yelling at him while he was up working on the roof. As soon as I was able to walk and talk I would follow on the heels of my uncles, father, grandfather, hired hands, even total strangers, and would assist them in whatever task was at hand. The problem was I would inquire every few seconds how much faster the work was going because I was helping. And I wouldn't accept generic statements of quantification but would demand specific answers, though well-reasoned estimates were acceptable, as to the extent of my assistance vis-a-vis the overall timetable to finish the job.

On the day George went up on the garage roof he apparently had done so to escape me and decided to derive solitude from altitude. For some reason a hammer came down from the roof and hit me on the head as I was running around in circles on the ground below. It knocked me unconscious. I remember coming to and asking George how such a thing could have happened. Every time I fingered the lump on my head for the next few days, I had a nagging suspicion it wasn't an accident in the purest sense. Even a little kid doesn't have to get hit on the head with a hammer to figure out life can be full of mystery.

During our adult discussion, George didn't come right out and admit he had dropped the hammer on my head by means of a deliberate act. He did, however, remind me that, in the course of his leisure reading, he had come across a statement attributed to the famous Dr. Sigmund Freud that there are no accidents. We left it at that and the subject never came up again.

From all of the above, the reader might begin to suspect that I was the ultimate uncoordinated klutz, but this was not the case. I think I was just a little bit accident prone. As a teenager I acquired substantial motor skills and hand-eye coordination. I was a good curler and not too bad a baseball pitcher. As a knife thrower I was a wizard. I transformed a World War I bayonet into a throwing knife with which I became deadly accurate. I would sneak up on a tree or a power pole, then hurl the bayonet where it would stick and then quiver. I could shoot with a bow and arrow, and was preternaturally skilled with a .22 single-shot Cooey rifle. I could also ride my bicycle backwards. I would sit on the handlebars facing the rear of the bike and then pedal at a rapid rate. I never fell or ran into anything.

One day I was coming down a hill on the bike, backwards as usual, with Ray Lovlin sitting on the seat, facing backwards too, and we almost hit Dr. Dwan's wife, Sheila, who was nearly nine months pregnant. She went into labour later that evening and delivered a healthy child, which I presume was not a boy, since it wasn't named after either Ray or me.

# Summer Scams (and some are just plain goofy)
## Dwayne W. Rowe

For those who lived in town, summers spent on a farm were the dangerous season. For someone who had been cooped up in a semi-urban community over an endless winter, the months of July and August provided an outlet for stored mischief. One of the most significant freedoms to be exercised was the right to pee outside. The framers of our new Charter of Rights and Freedoms prattled on about liberty, equality, the right to confront one's accusers and to receive a fair trial according to due process of law. But for the rural folk, a distinct society, there is no inherent bed-rock constitutional guarantee to be able to pee outside. Despite the lack of entrenchment of that precious liberty today, it was a de facto right forty years ago. It was so often claimed by me and my cousins at the farm that Grandad used to find his way out to the barn at night by following the yellow brick road. Actually, it was dirt but the point was well taken.

There is something cloying and claustrophobic about the

limitations of porcelain and, with all due respect to Sir John Crapper, inventor of the flush toilet, this convenience has its place but cannot be permitted to override a natural instinct dictating behaviour over millions of years.

Despite the fact that Grandad paid us well, in fact too much, for the minimal productive work we did around the farm, we were always aware of the need to raise extra cash. Our overhead consisted of .22 bullets, pop, licorice plugs and bike repairs. One method of generating revenue involved going to the Agricultural Fairgrounds at 4:00 AM, after a big wedding dance, and picking up hundreds of empty beer bottles, which sold for twenty cents a dozen. The problem arose when we attempted to take the bottles to the only depot in town. After riding five miles on bikes on gravel roads with gunnysacks of bottles hanging from the handlebars, the arrival at the depot was like landing on the beaches at Normandy. Nobody wanted to be first. The depot was a private home and garage. The lady in charge glowered, screamed, whined about dirt on the bottles, and had a countenance that resembled a mud fence in the rain.

The beer bottle game wasn't worth the candle, so we decided to develop another source of cash flow. On the farm at North Star one had to travel down a hill, cross over a dried-up creek, and then proceed up the other side to go to the village centre, which was basically a store and the community hall. Dances of all kinds and description were held in the hall and a lot of drinking went on outside. The men stepped out back to have a few drinks of extremely cheap whiskey and to go pee — an early form of recycling. My cousin Brian and I would stay up on dance nights and would take pails of water and wet down both sides of the slope leading to and from the tiny creek. Once the water was applied we would spin up and down the hill with our rubber boots to create a slippery surface. When the orchestra took a break at midnight, my dad, uncles, grandfather and their friends would head back to the farmhouse for a few drinks and some fine Swedish herring. Usually, this group would be displaying varying symptoms of impairment. When they hit the hill they, or if we were lucky, all of the men would slip on the wet ground and fall down. The obvious blame lay with the dangerous footing and not the effects of the demon drink — so they would pick themselves up and proceed to the house where more drinks would be consumed. On the way back to the dance they would fall again, and then again on the way home when the dance had ended. My cousin Brian and I would attend the scene and scoop up the loose change and sometimes paper money that had fallen out of their pockets as they fell down on their backsides. It was like a trapline and we checked it two or three times a night depending on the traffic.

Our best catch was the night the treasurer of the raffle committee slid down the hill on his butt, tearing his pocket, and the discovery of the trail of quarters shimmering in the moonlight was one of the most precious moments of our lives as, with greedy little fingers, we picked up each one of the shiny gems from the mud. It was like following the path to the end of the rainbow. We worked this scam for years until we were old enough to go to the dances ourselves. For some reason the only thing they never tumbled to was the truth. It seems to me the laws of nature would dictate that a sudden cloudburst wouldn't hit the same forty feet of creekbed every dance night for five years.

We hated rainy nights when the hill was wet on its own and sometimes stayed in bed and didn't bother to check the trapline. It would have been like getting a government grant not to farm. Our only regret came from the fact there was no local drycleaner, as it would have been a natural tie-in for a business deal of mutual advantage.

We used to harvest caragana seeds and try to sell them to the neighbours, all of whom had massive, uncontrolled forests of the stuff overtaking their yards. We tried to convince people the seeds were a good investment — a hedge against inflation — but the enterprise went the way of a canola-crushing plant thirty years later without the crushing debt.

We sold magazines like the *Saturday Evening Post* and *Popular Mechanics*. The best ones were *True Confessions* which had achingly sexy illustrations inside. After we had loaded up the family and their friends with longterm subscriptions (some of which have yet to expire), the market was saturated – the very concept of saturation soon turned our minds back to the slippery slope at the creek. We realized we had no option but to turn once more to our Department of Wet Affairs in order to produce some cash.

The community hall doubled as the movie house and a travelling projectionist would come up from Peace River on Friday nights. Some of our best ideas were adapted from the movies. We were able to insert a loaded mousetrap into a tobacco can so when Oscar reached inside his Old Chum to roll a smoke it would nail the end of his finger. We put water in bowls on the second shelf of the cupboard so when they were taken down the person got soaked. We got into Oscar's bottle of scotch and kept watering it down so badly he finally confronted us and told us if we were going to steal then go ahead and steal but forget about adding any liquid. We figured out that if he knew about it then it wasn't theft, much like the tree falling in the forest with nobody around to hear it crash.

We were confident we were actually stealing Spud cigarettes from Grandad's pack. The menthol nearly gagged us but it kept away summer colds. From the cowboy movies we learned how to loosen the seat on a bike and to tie a rope from it to a tree so when the rider jumped on and pedalled into the sunset, he did really well until he hit the end of the rope and the bike saddle flew off. We hitched my dog, Pal, to a wagon and then tied cousin Terry inside. Unfortunately, Pal chased trucks and, when he spotted a big semi passing the farm gate, he took off in pursuit. Terry was rocking back and forth inside the wagon screaming, as Pal, over the course of a hundred yards, drew up to the rear of the big dual tires on the trailer and starting snapping at the valve stems. My Aunt Anna was very unhappy about this but it hasn't hurt Terry one bit. He is now a senior vice-president of a large Canadian airline and I like to think he is where he is today because of the adversity faced in his formative years. A bonus is that, after being a bound hostage on a terrifying wagon ride, he has absolutely no fear of flying. Even the flakiest pilot isn't a tire-biter.

There comes a time when the limit is near. The beginning of the end was when Brian and I had seen a terrific cowboy-and-Indian movie at the hall. The cavalry were riding across what seemed to be empty desert. Suddenly, the ground opened up and hundreds of warriors rose from beneath the sand to attack the soldiers. We realized the technique could be adapted to our farm.

In those days everyone had an outhouse. On the path to this building we dug up the ground and created a hole about three feet deep just in front of the privy door. Then we filled the hole with water. The painstaking part was to cover the hole with thin boards from old apple boxes and to replace the dirt and sod on top so the surface of the ground looked undisturbed. It had to be a work of immense precision because our victim would not be on horseback scanning the horizon for Apaches but on foot looking at the ground. Within an hour or so, Uncle George came roaring out of the house, obviously in distress, heading for the privy. He was at top speed when he stepped on the path where the boards lay under the sod and he crashed into the watery grave. The trap had worked beyond expectations.

The oversight was in forgetting that George was a veteran of WWII. When he arose, mud-covered, out of that trench I was as scared as I have ever been in my life. Those eyes! He looked like Rocket Richard bearing down on the hated Maple Leafs as he came toward our inadequate hiding place. We escaped to a cave on the creek bank about two miles from home and lived on berries and chocolate bars for the first day. On the second day Grandad brought us food and a few Spud cigarettes. We realized it was his way of telling us a couple of things: he knew about the cigarette thefts and he couldn't smooth over the Apache Trap Incident. We discussed an apology, unconditional surrender, even internment in a camp as means of solving the impasse, but George was holding out for death by strangling.

Brian and I talked it over after Grandad left, and decided George was being unreasonable. On the afternoon of the third day at our outlaw hole-in-the-bank hideout it started to rain. The creek rose to the entrance of the cave. Death by drowning is preferable to having the seeds squeezed out of one's Adam's apple so we stayed put. About suppertime George appeared at the top of the bank and told us to come on into the house, that we had suffered enough. Grandad had obviously worked out some kind of amnesty on the condition we not bug George for the next ten years. Anyone who seriously believes the death penalty is not an effective deterrent to crime or practical jokes has never stood quaking and shivering in our boots.

After that period of terror, the only recidivist act I remember committing was when I threw a large potato at Oscar who was hoeing some hills at least a hundred feet away. It hit him square in the middle of the forehead. He passed out and his two-hundred-pound deadweight snapped the hoe handle. As I was heading over to see how he was doing, he unfortunately revived. Clutching the remnants of the hoe handle, he came at me. I was about fifteen at the time and he was nearly forty, but at the end of the next quarter section I looked over one shoulder and Oscar was about three feet behind, that big Swedish right arm swinging the handle at the base of my skull. If he hadn't passed out again I think he would have got me.

There came a point when I gave up on the dumb childhood gags and leaned more toward the mental frauds. I remember one day when Dad and I were in the car parked in front of the drugstore. He went in for something and when he returned I affected a downcast look, in fact a pout. When asked what was wrong, I told Dad that all the kids had Easter masks except me.

"What in hell is an Easter mask?" he asked. I explained that it was a new fad. Dad got out of the car and went back into the store. I could see him at the back talking to Arlie Bruder, the pharmacist. He was gesturing and pointing and putting his hands over his face to pantomime a mask. I watched Arlie take Dad over to the Easter egg and chocolate bunny section, but Dad kept on using his hands to indicate he was looking for a mask. Arlie kept shaking his head. Dad came out and got back into the car. He looked at me with the cold, grey eyes of a highschool principal, which he had been for a lifetime, and said through his teeth, "There are no goddamned Easter masks."

Why did I do such things? Why did Ray Lovlin and I decide to fart into empty milkbottles before returning them to Jimmy Eggenberger's store. We stuffed our mitts in the neck of the bottles to hold in the vile gases and once inside the store pulled the plug, so to speak, and put the bottles right under the big overhead heater hanging from the ceiling over the cash register. The outside temperature was about forty below zero and the inside was about eighty above so the expansion of the previously trapped vapours was probably a thousand to one. Jimmy was at the cash register tallying up for a nice lady from the United Church. When the odor hit them, she scurried away to get a jar of pickles at the back of the store. Jimmy called over one of his clerks and spoke to him. We could see the kid denying it, but Jimmy was the boss and made him put on his coat and stand outside for about ten minutes. Unfortunately the advent of the milk carton has rendered this gag obsolete.

Most of us had slingshots and shot each other with navy beans. I went through three pair of lenses in my glasses in one year. It is obviously a paranoia-producing chromosome that causes mothers always to tell their kids, "Be careful, you're going to take somebody's eye out."

Ray and I got into a cache of ballbearings and used them for serious shooting. Again, in January — but it was always

January in that town — we were walking home and suddenly stopped and drew our slingshots. We loaded each with a ballbearing and took aim on the power transformer where we had spotted a Nazi sniper about to rain death on some passerby. We fired our weapons from about one hundred yards and one or both the missiles obviously struck the enemy marksman but, unfortunately, richocheted onto the big glass insulator on the transformer. Since the temperature was at its usual level, that is, approaching absolute zero, the insulator shattered into bits. The street lights were the first to go out and then the whole town went dark. It took the entire night for the power crew to repair the damage. Ray and I never revealed our act of heroism in eradicating the last Nazi soldier. It is possible he escaped in the darkness but, to the best of our knowledge, there were never any more sniper attacks in our town.

# The Funniest Thing...
## Hal C. Sisson

My memory is very good. In fact, I can remember something that happened before I was born. I can recall going to a picnic with my father and coming home with my mother.

Now you will only accept on faith what you know cannot be true. Although I can dredge that thought up from the depths of my memory, I cannot remember to whom it may be credited. Many have had that same thought about faith, as there is much in religion that the intelligent mind refutes.

To overlook the humourous aspects of the world's innumerable religions is a mistake, and in the West we are primarily concerned with the three great religions which sprang from the same source in the Middle East, namely Islam, Judaism and Christianity — whose followers fight continually over their not so dissimilar versions of the same God. The quarreling between them stems from their past politics, their greed, bigotry, intolerance, and the religious arrogance of their various interpretations of a common religious history. They all have internal sects within their own religions, who hate each other, and each major religion hates its rivals. Having more to gain for humanity by amalgamation, they remain steadfastly separate and deadly enemies regardless of the lip service they may pay to brotherly love and tolerance.

And proselytize — my God, how all religions love to gain converts, but if one of their own goes over to another religion they are guilty of betrayal. "I have faith," said Sydney J. Harris, "but you live in a fool's paradise." But all churches need adherents and money to survive. I was listening to a Toronto television station a short time ago — Box so and so, Station U, Toronto, Ontario — an evangelist with a bad rug, a rumpled suit and an unfortunate speaking voice was haranguing the church stalwarts in the captive TV audience. "To Win the Lost at Any Cost!" was his motto. "Let's finish the work for Jesus — who is coming again soon (to another theatre near you, I suppose). If you don't tithe and send the money in to this ministry, you'll regret it. You have some of God's money! Now send it in!"

I seem to recall that Jesus was anti-orthodox and turfed the moneychangers out of the temple, although his motive escapes me. Probably figured the priests were in abrogation of their fiduciary duty to the parishioners. Ripping them off, as it were, and Jesus didn't go in for that crap. So are you going to send money in to a religious TV huckster? Why not? A sucker is born every minute, and many must mail in the dough or they wouldn't still be on the air. It is black humour, but still funny.

What was the funniest thing I ever saw live in an actual church service? Because I did go to church for a long time during the brainwashed days of my youth. It was in the United Church in Mount Forest, Ontario. The Reverend Pratt had been the longtime pastor at Zion United Church in Moose Jaw. His second oldest son, Mel, was my best buddy, and a few months before we graduated from high school, Reverend Pratt had been transferred to Mount Forest. In the summer of 1940, Mel and I hitchhiked down

East. It was easy in those days, as no one was afraid to pick up young strangers. I stayed in Ontario, got a job in Toronto and often visited the Pratts. Preachers' sons tend to shy away from church-going if they can — and so did I — but when you are a guest in the minister's home, you attend church service on Sunday morning. Norm Pratt, the youngest son, and I did just that, and on this occasion, there was a guest preacher of some note on hand to deliver the sermon.

He and the Reverend Pratt occupied the two high-backed heavy oak chairs on the dais, behind and on either side of the pulpit. Red plush on the seats and arms, castors on the legs. The floor of the speaking platform was of wood and had no railings. Rev. Pratt began his introduction of the guest speaker, and he was praising his qualifications to the skies. The visiting dignitary was making self-deprecatory body movements on his throne and, as a consequence, his chair, already too close to the edge, was moving on its castors. One leg was coming dangerously close to the edge of the dais. I leaned over to Norm and whispered, "He'd better not do too much more of that." But he did. One chair leg suddenly slipped off the edge of the platform and the chair toppled into the space in front of the congregation, throwing the preacher into the first row of pews. He literally flew through the air with the greatest of ease, glanced off a couple of parishioners, hit the back of the pew, then thudded onto the floor of the church. For a moment there was dead silence, then came the involuntary laugher, followed immediately by cries of concern. You could break your neck in a fall like that.

The Rev. cried out from the pulpit, "Are you all right, Jack (or whatever his name was)?" I'll give that parson credit, because, although he must have been hurting like hell as he lay flat on his back in the aisle, he said he thought he was not injured and slowly raised himself to a sitting position, as everyone sat stunned in their pews.

Upon receipt of this information, whether correct or not, the Reverend Pratt intoned, "What man shall there be among you, that shall have one sheep, and if it fall into a pit on the sabbath day, will he not lay hold on it, and lift it out? Matthew 12:11." A couple of ushers started down the aisle.

"And David said unto God, I am in great and dire straits," came the riposte from the preacher on the floor, "let me fall now into the hand of the Lord; for his mercies are great: and let me not fall into the midst of men. Second Samuel 24:14."

"You seem to have already done so," was Pratt's reply to this biblical sally. "But pride goeth before destruction, and a haughty spirit before a fall. Proverbs 16:18." The congregation was by this time laughing uproariously. Norm and I were nearly rolling in the aisles ourselves.

"Let us not judge one another anymore," the decked pastor said, rising to his knees, "but judge this rather, that no man put a stumbling block or an occasion to fall in his brother's way. Romans 14:13." More laughter.

"A word fitly spoken is like apples of gold in pictures of silver. Proverbs of Solomon 25:11," said Pratt, not to be outdone.

"Wherefore let him that thinketh he standeth take heed lest he fall. First Corinthians 10:12. I have fallen, but I shall now try to rise again — with great difficulty!" And the guest minister got up and walked slowly back onto the dais while members of the congregation lifted the oak chair back into place. For a short while they had been religious standup comics, and if they had done it every week they could have filled the church for a long run. The guest even de-voted part of his sermon to Proverbs 29:23 — "A man's pride shall bring him low: but honour shall uphold the humble in spirit."

Funniest thing I ever saw or heard in a church service.

Which naturally starts one to thinking— what was the funniest thing I ever experienced in a movie theatre? It wasn't the time at the Edmonton Garneau Theatre when I saw the sneak preview of *Ice Palace* — a turgid three-hour saga of three generations of an Alaskan pioneer family. The movie finally came to the point in history where Don Ameche had invented the telephone. And when one of the first telephones in Alaska rang in the movie, I got up from my seat and said, "I think that's for me!" and worked my way down the row to the aisle and out, to laughter and applause.

By coincidence, the funniest occasion also involved Mel Pratt. This time in the Famous Players Capitol Theatre in Moose Jaw, Saskatchewan. You will remember the 3D movies, the ones where they issued you a set of glasses with which to view those special effects movies. Everything looked like it was coming right off the screen at you. Every so often the non-existent plot called for a baseball pitcher to seemingly throw his pitch right at your head, or an arrow to fly from a bow in the same manner. Mel and I, high school students, went on a Saturday afternoon. One segment of the 3D movie involved a fire and the inevitable arrival of the firemen and the hose — which of course they turned toward the audience, amid shrieks of excitement from the kids.

My friend and I, however, had come armed with water pistols!

We were seated in front of a mother and her young boy — maybe he was about five years old. We placed our loaded pistols under our armpits pointing to the rear, right at the kid. When the time arrived in the movie for the firemen to do the hose bit, we let him have it with both barrels, as it were. He was getting a good soaking and was yelling, "Momma, Momma, I'm getting all wet!"

"Shut up!" the mother was telling him. "It's only a movie."

But still the kid of course persisted. He was getting wet and complaining loud and long about it to his mother. Finally she stopped berating him and checked the child out. Sure enough, he was all wet. She grabbed him by the hand, rushed him into the aisle and out into the lobby, where she began yelling for the manager. Mel and I followed, having no desire, as hit men, to remain at the scene of the shooting.

The manager was at a complete loss. He could see the kid was all wet but how could he get that way? He tried suggesting that the kid had peed himself with excitement, but the mother was having none of that — "It doesn't smell like pee and how could he pee himself all over his jacket and arms?" was her reply. We didn't want to be seen laughing that hard until we got out in the street, so we had to leave them arguing in the lobby. The last I heard was the manager offering the mother her money back. That movie in the late thirties was before its time — they are not making them that realistic even yet.

# Baseball in its own Slanguage
Hal C. Sisson

*A loaf of bread and a pound of meat,*
*And all the mustard you can eat!*

The smell of peanuts filled the air as you watched the hot-dog vendors hawk their products in the old-time ballparks. My brother Ted played in the alfalfa ball loops of Western Canada in mid-century. His stuff included both smoke and junk and he pitched to a lot of willow-wielding marble thumpers in his time. No better than he thought he was, but no horsehide Houdini, his performances ranged between sky-high blowups and two-hitters.

No crooked arm sidewinder, Ted, just a journeyman rightpaw, who did all right when he had his stuff — which ranged from a burnt offering scorcher to what he called his nothing ball. He maintained he had a hook which he had to throw at third base in order to get it across home plate, and a knuckler that was so slow that the first baseman could run in and autograph the ball before it crossed the pan.

Actually his best pitch was high and inside, and when he faced a batter who crowded the plate, he could dust him back like a scalded dog. In some games, this made him about as popular as a turd in a punch bowl.

In my recollection, the worst game Ted ever pitched was one he started in Eckville. After he hit five of the first six batters, the hometown fans got noisier than a mule in a tin barn. Little old ladies crowded the baselines, calling him a murderer and demanding his immediate removal. The situation got rougher than goat guts and we had to fight our way back to the car and head for the hills like big-assed birds. Never been so close to a lynch mob before. Uncle Murray was shaking so much he couldn't have taken a crap in a ten-acre field. Ted had the wrong stuff that day.

Pitching, in my opinion, often depends on whether you are facing a murderer's row of pellet pounders, a bunch of powder puffs who swing like your little sister, or goops who make like Babe Ruth in practice but can't hit their hat size in a game.

I remember Ted pitching a no-hitter up to the eighth stanza, the only problem being that the other pitcher was doing the same. In the ninth chapter he four-balled a suspected clouter to first, then dusted back the next hickory hammerer, causing a rhubarb. The next batter hit a daisy clipper through the infield and this scooter beat out the throw to first; then burglarized second, putting runners on second and third. With two down, one of his pasture patrol turned into a juggler and dropped the final out, allowing two runs to score. That was the ball game.

On another occasion his Red Deer team was in tough against Butte, Montana. The opposing pitcher was ambidextrous, and pitched the first three innings as a southpaw. In the fourth he suddenly went over to the dugout and changed gloves, then pitched the rest of the game with his right arm. Just as good from either side. My brother hardly ever talked about that game — his team was already trailing by several counters and the bases were loaded. Red Deer's starting screwballer, plus another pitcher, had already been shelled from the mound and given the hook by the coach. Now the coach calls Ted in from the orchard and says, "Do something about this mess. Clean it up!"

Ted took the ten warm-up pitches that are allowed and then faced the next apple knocker for the opposition as he stood pawing the dirt at home plate. Ted shook off a signal from his catcher for a red hot rivet, decided his first pitch would be his sinker, and wound up the old soup bone. The pill forgot to drop and came up fat and juicy right in the centre of the pan. The batter swung the old eggbeater for an out of park homer, four runs scored and the bases were cleared.

Ted came off the mound, walked over to the coach and said, "Well, coach, I got that cleaned up. What do you want me to do next?"

Lucky thing my Uncle Murray wasn't umping that afternoon. However, he did do the three blind mice bit around Red Deer from time to time. On one occasion at Sylvan Lake, the crowd was really onto him, giving him a terrible roasting for his decisions. He did wear glasses, which didn't help his umpire image as you can imagine. But I thought that remarks like "hick with a white stick," and "You're the first blind man I seen who don't have a dog," went a little too far and were uncalled for.

Well, came the seventh inning stretch, and when everyone was again seated and the ball players all ready to start, there was no sign of the umpire. Murray was nowhere to be seen. A long minute passed — my uncle's timing was always good. Everyone was looking for the ump and the natives were starting to get restless.

Suddenly, Uncle Murray stood up near the top of the bleachers along the third base line and yelled at the top of his lungs, "PLAY BALL!" All heads turned toward him as he continued, "PLAY BALL! APPARENTLY YOU CAN SEE THINGS BETTER FROM UP HERE!" And that is what he did. He called the rest of that ball game from the stands — strikes, balls, safe or out, he called them all from the third base bleachers. The crowd gave him a standing ovation at the end of the game.

# Blaze of Glory

### Dwayne W. Rowe

The Battle River country was rich in sporting events. We had a baseball league with teams from Manning, Hotchkiss, Deadwood, Dixonville, Warrensville and Grimshaw. Later on, the Deadwood franchise moved to North Star. The Deadwood Dodgers were the equivalent of the New York Yankees and their manager, Paul Schuster, was as close as I ever got or will get to the kind of baseball wizardry found in Casey Stengel.

Our Manning team started out as the Wheat Kings, but, after a few bad crop years with smut and drought and frost, we changed our name to the Comets, figuring it was better to burn to death in a blaze of glory than lie around the field and rot or freeze. For the most part, we were a collection of high school kids playing against men.

The Dodgers were farmers with thick wrists, bulging biceps, fantastic reflexes and 20-20 vision. The oldest guy on our team was twenty-one and a lot of us, especially myself, were uncoordinated four-eyed geeks. At age fifteen I wasn't strong enough to overpower a batter, so I developed pretty good control together with a knuckleball that, on a good day, you could read the brand name all the way from the mound to the plate.

I like to think we did beat the Dodgers but cannot recall the exact details of the victory. Ordinarily, one would expect the big win to be forever etched in the brain, but as the years passed and I read everything I could lay hands on that was written by Roger Kahn, Roger Angell and W.P. Kinsella, the mystical properties of the game evoked by those geniuses have become inextricably bound up with my own memories of playing in our league.

Apart from Paul Schuster, who had the talent to manage anywhere, the Dodgers had a player, Chester Reinders, who could do it all. He could hit, run, throw and was a great catcher. Behind that plate he dominated the field. I tried to steal second one day and he fired the ball to the second baseman, who had it in his glove while I was still too far away for him to recognize my facial features. He laughed so hard he dropped the ball and I slid on by him and would have been safe except for being about three feet off line.

Sometimes the mosquitoes were so bad in the outfield grass that, when Chester came up to bat and I was pitching, I'd walk him intentionally so my outfielders wouldn't run around and stir up black clouds of the killer insects which would bug them the rest of the game. We could never get the hang of the fancy signals the Dodgers used so we just let our third-base coach stand there and scratch wherever he liked. Since our base-runners were pretty much undisciplined anyway, when a play looked as though it were deliberate it used to drive Paul Schuster crazy. He'd work all week changing the signals for the next weekend games and once accused one of his second string players of talking too much over a few beers.

I remember Old "Casey" Schuster marking on a diagram of the diamond the exact spot where opposing players would hit the ball during each game. Apparently there was an immutable pattern which emerged every season. The Comets were an exception. We were raw kids trying to swing those long, heavy bats against pitchers who could throw a pail of milk sixty feet let alone a baseball. One guy from Warrensville, Herman Wolski, had one pitch, a vicious fastball that hummed as it rose, usually high, hurtful and definitely inside. He could stick that thing in a teacup at fifty paces or inside an ear or eye socket. Swinging against Herman was an act of desperation, a convulsive shrinking away from disaster and any contact with the ball usually meant it could land anywhere. One time, one of our boys made pretty good contact but had shied away so badly, he was facing third at the time so he dropped the bat and ran to the nearest base. Which by itself wasn't all bad except that our coach was scratching his nuts at the time and accidentally triggered a hit-and-run play so the fellow on third headed for home and clobbered the batter about halfway.

There was no fence around the field and foul balls and wild throws would hit the spectators' cars and break the windshields. A lot of times we never kept track of our stats, but I do know one weekend at Dixonville we broke four windshields out of forty times at bat which is about .100 in any league.

The season was short so we played double-headers on Sundays and entered a lot of tournaments. We played on Farmers' Day, July 1st, the opening day at the Fair and any other excuse. Top prize money was $250 which might as well have had the Dodgers name already filled in on the cheque. But, the Comets did pick up some cash along the way from coming in second or third. We used to buy a few bats and balls and then spend the rest on beer. Mostly we bought Calgary Stock Ale because it had an alcohol content that, by today's standards, would be outlawed.

At a tournament at Bear Lake we were doing pretty well and got into the finals against the Dodgers. We knew it was pointless but had to show up to claim the second prize money. We were sleeping in tents and it was cold, so we stayed up all night drinking beer. The next day the sun came out and, by game time, it was hotter than hell. Vern Money, our centrefielder, had an incredible hangover and basically couldn't see at all. I was pitching and the arm was loose. I got the first two batters on strikeouts and an error put the next guy on first. Chester Reinders, batting in his usual clean-up position, came to the plate. I decided to give him the knuckeball on the theory that even if he clobbered it, the goofiness of the pitch was such it would be a mushy pop-up or a dribbler along the ground.

I wasn't all that strong, but I was a thinking pitcher. Obviously, I got some spin on the damn thing and Chester nailed it in mid-rotation. It went over my head and I could hear it screaming out to the horizon. Vern Money, ever alert, must have picked up the sound or the movement and yelled, "I got it, I got it." The ball was in level flight, still gaining speed, when it hit Vern right between the eyes. The guy on first and Chester had both crossed home by the time we ran out to see how Vern was doing. A lump the size of an orange had formed between the bridge of his nose and forehead and he just lay there and moaned about how that Calgary Stock Ale was horse-piss and always gave him a headache.

It never was our day against the hated Dodgers but a couple of innings later we did tie it up and things were looking good. Even Vern, who was now assigned to third-base coaching duties, was starting to sense the victory and the first prize money. He told me later he could almost taste the Stock Ale sliding down his throat. At the bottom of the sixth inning my knuckleball got away from me and dropped like a stone onto the plate. Unfortunately, it bounced back at an angle so as to get under the catcher's cup and he threw off his mask and rolled around in the dirt clutching his balls. Vern started to laugh and it made his head hurt so bad he threw up. Our manager, Albert McClarty, pulled me and sent in Jimmy Brick, a real fire-baller. It wasn't Jimmy's fault but the momentum was lost and so was the game.

Afterwards we had a few beers with the Dodgers. One of the Scandinavian players, a "Scandahoovian" as we called it, was bugging Jimmy about being part native. Jimmy finished his beer, stood up to his full six foot six inches and told him, "A thousand Swedes ran through the weeds, chased by one big Indian." Paul Shuster came over and cooled things off by explaining his latest theories and everybody's eyes glazed over, even those who only had one Stock Ale.

Being an umpire was a thankless job, but Pete Schroh could handle it better than most. One game, Pete was umping and the ball went by the catcher and hit Pete in the head. He fell down, lay still for a moment, then got up and started cursing. Mike Fetiuk, who had been umping at third, ran up to Pete and declared, "I knew you wasn't dead when I heard you talkin'." At that point even Doc Lambert agreed with the diagnosis and the game continued.

One of our boys made it to what was pretty close to the bigs. Ray Lovlin got a baseball scholarship to UCLA and played on the same team as Ron Fairly, who went on to the other Dodgers and later to Montreal. One of my catchers, Father George Fetsch, was constantly in trouble with his senior parishioners because he wore his Comets uniform under his cassock and would cut Mass real short in order to go play ball with us Protestants. I'll never forget the time he got called out on a third strike, standing there looking, which is enough to make anybody commit a few venial sins, and he was nearly apoplectic when he managed to spit out, "Horse...feathers." From then on, every time he came up to bat in that town, somebody would holler out, "Father Horsefeathers, I think your bat is holey."

My affections remain unchanged over the years for Ernie McClarty, our regular catcher, who was the old man on the team at age twenty-one and could have played with another team but felt we were so pitiful, somebody had to look after us. I also owe a lot to his father, Albert, who got me interested in the game and gave me a chance to play. After three or four years, when other things began to get in the way of baseball, I wasn't quite so much of a geek and had learned to love the game and the people who play it. Sometimes I think I would like to recall a lot of names of those guys in the league, but then I remember the hits they got off me, and like any pitcher who ever threw a ball in competition, there is a kind of quick, searing hatred of those bastards and it takes a second or so to pass. When it does, I feel all warm and mooshy and a bit like a geek, which starts the whole cycle rolling again in an endless unchanging loop, and I can feel the sweat between the ribs and memorize the sneer on Casey's weathered mug as my boys behind me chat it up, "He's done — he's gone — shoot him down," and the knuckleball floats in high and fat and catches a puff of wind before sliding across and down into the mitt, untouched by the now artless but still hateful Dodger.

# The Postman Cometh Twice
## Hal C. Sisson

You could dance in Airforce issue boots but not very well. So I saved up for a pair of quarter Wellington, plain black shoes which I would wear on leave or if out on the town. Occasionally, keen officer types of the air or other forces would notice this and take umbrage, demanding to know why I should be wearing non-issue footwear. They were the type that brooked no variance from the set dogma of rules and regulations — the peacetime military mind wants nothing to interfere with complete obedience to the standing or any other orders given to the private shock troops. How else could they get them to fix bayonets and charge into point blank machine gun fire. Personally, I always wondered how drunk I would have to be to do that?

Anyway, if accosted and taken to task re the shoes, there were several ploys one could use. "The medical officer has ruled that, due to a left foot injury caused during bomb loading, a lighter boot with a longitudinal arch support was necessary." The more experienced military bureaucrat might not buy this, in which case you had to choose between merely doing a bunco from the scene (in lighter shoes you could likely outrun them), or, as a last resort, telling them that you would never wear the shoes again if they would just forget about it this time. If they believed that story they would believe anything. What did they expect you to do with the shoes in that case? Throw them away? Give them to the Sally Ann? The officers already had a better class of footwear and the other non-commissioned ranks such as sergeants or warrant officers were already brain-washed, so they were all for full-out compliance.

It was the same with sheets. If you tried to sleep in anything else but rough forces-issue blankets, some inspecting officers got really uptight. So I often had to hide the sheets I had received from home in my locker. The fact that you might like a little comfort if you could get it was beside the point in His Majesty's Forces, who figured Spartan conditions bred tougher troops. The times I got into trouble or on charge were mostly of this nature — flouting those kinds of rules and regulations.

I met Freddie Ryan at the RCAF Manning Depot in Brandon, Manitoba, and we were buddies for about two years. Too bad one can't retain the same friends throughout military service, but continual postings usually prevent that. An Irish boy who had been too young and too skinny to go with the Winnipeg regiment to Singapore, he grew a little older and put on some weight and joined the RCAF as a potential radio technician. A couple of things he told me have always stuck in my mind — and they illustrate the type of ingenuity necessary to make "walking around money" for a youth in the depression years.

Fred came from the South side of Winnipeg, not to be confused he said, with the much tougher and more famous North side. On the South side they also had their scams, however. Freddie told me about two that he had done when he was about twelve. He and a friend inserted an ad in one of the two-bit pulp adventure magazines which were popular in the thirties. The advertisement said, in effect: SYSTEMATIC INSECT KILLER! PRODUCT GUARANTEED TO KILL ANY BUG —*whether Aphid, Armybug, Caterpillar, Cutworm, Leafhopper, Mite, Spruce Bugworm, Stinkbug, Ant or Webworm! Fill in the form below and SEND ONLY 25¢. Include two five-cent stamps for immediate return of our AMAZING NEW PRODUCT!*

When the orders came in, Fred and his friend, Bryant DeBrule, placed two small thin blocks of wood marked "A" and "B" respectively, into an envelope, along with a note which set out the "Instructions for Use": "Take Block A in left hand and place the bug to be killed onto the block. Then take Block B in right hand and smash down on Block A."

Guaranteed to Kill any Bug!

The boys were doing very well financially until, one day, a Mountie knocked on the door of the Ryan residence looking for a Mr. Ryan. His father and mother being separated, Mrs. Ryan said she would fetch Freddie. When the cops found out he was only a kid, they considered his tender years and dropped the charges of defrauding through the mails which they had been prepared to lay. Personally I think he had a good defense —it would kill any bug. They told him not to do it again and his mother said, "He won't, and I will guarantee that!"

I don't know whether that was before or after she caught him herself in another bit of business he had going for him. This was a pay telephone route. You stuffed cotton batten up the coin return slot of the public pay phone so that the dimes made no noise when they were returned if your call was not completed. At regular intervals you then went over your route, checked your pay phones, removed the cotton and collected any money which had accumulated in the upper reaches of the slot. Fred's worst mistake was that of incorporating into his route the phones in the Hudson Bay Department Store — where his mother happened to be one of the store detectives.

It was hard for a kid to make walking around money in

the dirty thirties. I was not surprised in later life when Fred was asked to run the largest "OktoberFest" in Canada, in Kitchener, Ontario, and went on to become a very successful self-employed businessman.

So we had both signed up for the radio technicians course of the Royal Canadian Air Force, and after basic training at Brandon, were sent to McGill University in Montreal. There were 180 members in this class, and sixteen weeks of instruction were given in the fundamentals of electricity and magnetism, alternating current and radio. The course was designed essentially to provide an adequate number of radar technicians to maintain radio locators in Britain and other areas where radar was needed.

The placement officer had taken the attitude that, as I had passed grade twelve, I could show great aptitude in absorbing this instruction. I did, up to a point — but that point was very soon passed. As far as radar was concerned, I would still be sitting on a hot stove at sixty-five; I wouldn't have learned or understood a damned thing. It takes years to become a brain overnight; and some of the men could tear down a radio and put it back together before they ever arrived on that course. I should have told the Airforce that the subjects with which I had great difficulty were stuff like analytical geometry, chemistry and physics. You have to be both mechanically minded and interested to get the hang of things like Ohm's Law, the capacity of a parallel plate condenser, and the field intensity of a single loop coil in stat farads.

Fred Ryan and I stuck it out for six weeks because the Montreal girls were so pretty, but what the hell they were talking about on that course meant no more to me then than it does to me now. Luckily for the war effort, it was right down some other people's alley. On the last test they gave before sending us back to Toronto Manning Depot, there was one question asked which could be answered correctly. A problem was described and you were asked to state whether it was caused by weak or strong spark? We flipped a coin, heads you said weak and tails you took strong. Fred got two marks and I got zero. So much for radar training, but fate decrees that one thing always leads to another.

Meanwhile, back at Manning Depot, Freddie went downtown to see his father's former partner, Mr. Meyers, who ran the Meyers Photo Studios across Canada, with head office in Toronto. Mr. Meyers suggested we could likely sell a lot of photo coupons at the Manning Pool, at $1.00 a crack. The buyer was invited to attend at Meyers Studios and have his photo taken at a discount upon presentation of the coupon. The best part of this deal was that the sellers of the coupons, Freddie and I got to keep the entire buck on each sale. Everyone except the staff is a new recruit at a Manning depot; and Toronto was the largest of its kind, just jammed with the youth of Canada, all of whom seemed exceedingly anxious to send a picture of themselves in uniform back to the mother, wife or girlfriend at home. We did so well at this that neither Freddie nor I bothered to attend pay parade for the couple of months we were there waiting to remuster to another trade. Later we sold the exclusive Manning Depot Meyers Photo Coupon franchise to a couple of other guys —who undoubtedly did likewise when they had to leave. Fate decrees that one thing, one occurrence, inevitably leads to a sequel —which is not quite another tale, so I'll tell it anyway.

You did have a choice as to which side of your anatomy to let freeze —front or butt —as you sat huddled around the small, pot-bellied stove in a quonset hut in Castle Archdale, Northern Ireland. Art Ross was telling us, "You won't remember these damp, rotten, boring times when you look back on your service —you'll only remember the highlights, the great times, the escapades, the parties and the pub crawls, the times when something exciting happened." And he was right.

Two of those times I remember clearly because they involved being posted overseas. I did get there twice —on both occasions by a fluke, an aberration in the incompetent conduct of the war by the military experts who allegedly ran it. Not that they needed me in either instance, nor that the enemy wasn't given encouragement by those occurrences.

The first instance was to Alaska and here's how it came about that I was posted there. I couldn't make aircrew because of catarrh. I washed out of radar at McGill University —my mind never did cotton to an understanding of things mechanical or the workings of radio or physics. At Toronto Manning Pool, I tried to remuster into the journalistic, propaganda and/or entertainment section of the RCAF. I'd had some experience in the latter while M.C.ing the "Smiler's Concert Party" at Brandon Manning Depot. The third time I bugged him, the placement officer said no rookies need apply and, if I didn't make up my mind to sign up for instrument bashing or armament within twenty-four hours, he would be happy to assign me to general duties. Well, you don't want to spend the war sweeping hangars or working the silvermine in a messhall, that's for sure. And all the guys I was with at the time were going to take armament. So, still without much mechanical ability, I went along with them to Mountainview Airport in southern Ontario.

While there, learning to strip Browning machine guns and Hispano cannon, Freddie Ryan and I managed to get put on charge enough times to be on a first name basis with the sergeant in charge of the military police. Our course finished, posting time came around, and we met our MP friend in a Belleville beer parlour. He told us confidentially that he had a friend in the provost corp in Mossbank, Saskatchewan, who had very recently informed him that Hurricane Fighter Squadron #135 was finishing their training in that prairie metropolis of several hundred souls, and were about to be moved to Pat Bay on Vancouver Island. Now that was considered a choice destination, whereas I knew Mossbank from another movie, having grown up in southern Saskatchewan.

The Airforce method of posting was to write the names of all the places that needed men around the classroom blackboard, then ask the candidates to write down their first and second choices underneath. One of the few times you were ever asked for your opinion. No person in their right mind was going to choose Mossbank, Saskatchewan, possibly to spend the rest of their air force days. But had the sergeant been conning us? Did he have the correct information? Had he told anyone else? Freddie and I agonized over these weighty problems, and then wrote only one choice on the blackboard under Mossbank. No one else did likewise. Everything rode on the validity of our information from a cop by whom we had been disciplined on a couple of occasions, but who seemed to like us nevertheless.

We got shipped to Mossbank. When we got there courtesy of the CPR, Adjutant Jobin turned out to be an old Winnipeg buddy of Fred's dad. So when we checked into the squadron office, he says to me as Fred's friend, "Sisson, you're from Moose Jaw, I see. Well, we're moving to Pat Bay next Saturday. You won't be any good here in that short a time, so take the truck into town tomorrow morning and stay with your folks, and God help you if you aren't on that station platform at oh-nine hundred Saturday morning."

I spent one night on Mossbank airport!

The 135th Squadron spent six months in Pat Bay flying over the Empress Hotel to convince the Victorian dowagers at tea that they were safe from Japanese invasion. Then I think the brass got inebriated with the Americans one night, and it was decided to see how a Canadian fighter squadron would liaise with the Yanks on Annette Island, Alaska, a big staging area for the American Army on their way to the Aleutians.

That was overseas number one, where we spent six months in tents before we went back to Terrace, B.C., via Seal Cove, Prince Rupert. Now, it was not only rumour but a fact that the only way ground crew could get out of Western Air Command was to die. Alaska had been interesting, but Terrace was as bad as Mossbank, just more rain, snow and fog. So I inadvertently found another way out of the northern B.C. bush.

I preferred charges under the King's Rules and Regulations against Sergeant Plouffe, the second in command of the armament section. The army, navy and air force are not based on democratic principles, even though you might think that they were formed in defence of that very purpose. The military hates democracy. It doesn't like fair play or justice very well, either, and if you understand that from the start, you will get along a lot better. It is essentially class warfare based on rank. A buck private or LAC is expected to be shat upon from great heights by his superiors. And the first thing you will notice about any military court system is the smell of kangaroo. After having your cap and belt taken, you are marched in under guard and must stand rigidly at attention throughout the procedure. You may only speak when spoken to — which system, come to think of it, should maybe apply to lawyers.

But when I laid this charge I didn't expect the eventual results. Okay, so Sergeant Plouffe didn't like Freddie and he didn't like me, and who is to say if this animosity was unwarranted? But in his cups he made the mistake of divulging this aversion to a friend of mine. Basically what he said was, "Make no mistook, s'il vous plaît, but I am goin' to get dose Ryan and Seeson, dey are goin' to da digger for shure."

When informed that this base canard had issued from the lips of our beloved sergeant, in front of witnesses yet, I took the precaution of preparing sworn affidavits to that effect. And, as it turned out, this was a wise precaution, because shortly thereafter Plouffe made his move. Albeit what happened and the charges he laid were what was termed in the forces "chicken-shit," he arranged to have the MPs pick us up by the short and curlies for failure to report for duty at the armament section in the hangar. Therefore we were technically AWOL and were escorted to the digger, locked in a cell, placed *in durance vile*, where we languished for several hours until the arrival of the officer of the day. His was an onerous joe-job parceled out by the adjutant to whichever officer headed his own current shit list.

Part of this Officer's job was to tour the camp and see that all was in proper order. He would go into the airmen's messhall for instance, and ask if there were any complaints. And, of course, it was a mistake to say anything other than "no" to this ridiculous query, for if you did complain about the food, you were most likely to end up spud bashing for several days. The officer-of-the-day would also go into the digger and ask the same question of those of his fellow Canadian servicemen who were unfortunate enough to be incarcerated there. Which he did in this instance. And we told him, "We don't know why we are here. We signed up for barrack fatigue this morning, and were just about to get out of bed to start cleaning up when we were arrested and brought here, apparently on the orders of one Sergeant Plouffe."

Well, he had to look into it. And sure enough, because our defense was valid, he returned three-quarters of an hour later and instructed our immediate release, no charges being layable. At that point I interjected, "Sir, not so fast, please! That isn't the end of it, either in my book or the King's Rules and Regulations." And then I brought out my affidavits, told my story, and quoted the section of the Rules under which I maintained Sergeant Plouffe should be charged for maliciously and willfully planning a persecution of members of His Majesty's Forces. The officer-of-the-day had to agree that I had that right and, as we were already in the Provost Marshall's office, I proceeded to do so. The warrant officer in charge showed little enthusiasm, in fact was very displeased, but I insisted. The papers were typed up, and Freddie and I left.

A week passed, ten days — no news of any action on the part of the MP office. I went down to see the warrant officer in charge. He told me they were working on it. Another week went by — nothing. I made another visit. Still no action.

"I want to see the commanding officer," I said to the W.0.2 in charge.

"No, you don't," he replied.

"You can tell me I can't see him, or that you won't let me

see him," was my rejoinder, "but you cannot tell me I do not want to see him."
"And just why is that?" he asked.
"Because the verb 'want' indicates the subjective. I am the only one who can say what I actually want. It is an impossibility for me to tell you what you want, and conversely, you cannot tell me what I want."
"You are one smartass sonofabitch," was his response. "I'll tell you why you don't *want* to see him!"
"And why is that?" I asked.
"Because you are posted overseas tomorrow!"
And I was and I went. The RCAF posted my ass out of Terrace in record time. Within twenty-four hours I had a physical examination, a dental checkup, my kit brought up to snuff at equipment stores, and was issued a ticket on the CN iron horse that ran through Jasper, Edmonton, across the Prairies, through Toronto, on to Lachine in La Belle Province, and eventually from there to Halifax, where the *Ille de France* waited to take us all to Grenoch, Scotland, then to the Bournemouth staging area in England.
I had expected to be working on fighter aircraft, on which by now I was proficient. Instead, they sent me to 422 Squadron of Coastal Command in Castle Archdale in Northern Ireland —where they flew the revamped *China Clippers*, the magnificent Sunderland flying boats. Took a bit more servicing —three turrets with four Browning 303 machine guns in each, two fifty calibers in the nose, and the cook could fire a gas-operated Thompson sub-machine gun out the large galley windows. That was in addition to the depth charges which ran out on racks from bomb bays on each side of the aircraft. Not that anyone could bitch about that steak-and-eggs posting, and, in the war years, everyone in Ireland was friendly, north and south. The IRA had called a truce in the face of the greater terrorism being imposed by the Nazis. About every six weeks, groundcrew drew guard duty aboard one of the Sunderlands anchored out in Loch Erne, but there was never an incident of sabo-

tage. If the Irish Republican Army had showed up, maybe I could have talked them out of sinking the flying boat but I figured one man with a .303 wasn't worth a pinch of coonshat. Your best bet would be to fire several cartridges from the Verey pistol, strip down to your shorts, and start swimming for shore.

I'll grant you, when the RCAF railroaded me out of Terrace, B.C., they did give me a month's leave in Moose Jaw. But that was a requisite that they couldn't avoid or they would not likely have done so, because they were in a condition often described in the forces as being "pissed off!" From my viewpoint, in this instance, attempting to lay a charge against a superior rank did pay off. From their viewpoint, they solved an unwanted situation by posting me overseas. Now, from what I later observed, if I had tried that on an RAF station somewhere, their solution would have been drastically different. Being far more rank conscious, they would likely have charged and convicted me of conduct prejudicial to His Majesty's forces or some such crime, and sent me to the infamous Glasshouse for a few months to smarten me up and teach me some respect. Although we colonials weren't that undemocratic.

And that is how, for me, the air force postman rang twice.

# Born Again

Dwayne W. Rowe

My birth certificate says I was born in Notikewin, Alberta. Actually, I was born in the hospital in Manning, except there was no town of Manning at the time. My parents were living at North Star, which is five miles south of where Manning would have been had it been there. Notikewin was five miles north of the hospital where I entered the world and the post office was there. I once tried to explain this to a customs officer who had never before in his twenty-five years on the job seen the name Notikewin. Partway through my explanation he waved me on and, for the first time in my life, I wished I had something to smuggle.

North Star was settled as Little Prairie, which was the name given to it by my maternal grandfather, Oscar Nord. A bunch of Scandahoovians were sitting around having a few shots of whiskey and wanted to call the place Nord Star, but my grandfather wisely rejected the honour. Since it was located so far up the map it made your nose bleed, they decided on the name North Star. The place did well for about thirty years until after the war, which was always referred to as WWII.

An American chap by the name of Pat Craig decided he liked the look of the spot on the river where the hospital was located. He bought up some property and announced he was going to build a hotel which would have a beer parlour. The entire community immediately split into factions and the residents of North Star and Notikewin could read, if not the handwriting on the wall, then the yellow writing in the snow, and faced the fact the new town would bring the end to their little villages. Pat Craig propounded the name of the new place as Aurora but Ontario already had one, which is typical, and the name Manning was chosen to honour Ernest C. Manning, then Premier of Alberta. Citizens opposed to the beer parlour referred to the proposed town as Arsehola and, even after it was officially named Manning, the few people in the area who didn't vote for Social Credit still used that name.

The liquor license was granted and by the time the first draft came out of the tap a new town had sprung up in close proximity to the bar. A new school was built in Manning and my father was transferred from his duties as principal of the school at North Star to head up the new facility. We moved to Manning in the winter of 1949, which means it could have been anytime between October and June.

Although the distance was only five miles, it was like entering another world. North Star had a general store with a hitching post in front with troughs for the horses. In winter the farmers would come into the village in their cutters, which were sleighs made of wood or old car bodies. A stove inside would be blazing away and the smokestack would be giving off white clouds in the forty below air as the families, all bundled up, were drawn into the community by a team of horses. We had a barber shop and a hardware and another grocery store and a blacksmith and a community hall and, to the eyes of an eight year old boy, a whole bunch of other stuff that seemed enough. We had a shoemaker named Bert Saunders who was normal from the waist up but had fallen out a tree as a kid and stunted the growth of his legs. In addition to mothers yelling at their kids to " watch out or you'll take somebody's eye out," they would also holler up into a tree, "Get down here, right now. Do you want to end up like Bert?"

In Manning, building lots were surveyed and businesses started up overnight in order to accomodate the trade of people going to the bar to drink beer. The crafty merchants in North Star and Notikewin moved out in the middle of the night and, by morning, were doing business in Manning. Some people stayed behind, moreso in North Star than in Notikewin, so that by 1985 about twenty people still lived there. It is difficult to imagine today someone deciding to build a bowling alley in the middle of a field by Wainwright and everyone from Edmonton and Calgary pulling up and moving there so they could bowl. But, in fairness, it was just after the war and draft beer was a luxury. Towns throughout history have been started in pursuit of gold, diamonds, copper or as military bases. Fresh beer is as good a reason as any.

But, for a long time after 1949 there still was a North Star. The Nord family was there and wouldn't move the six quarter-sections just to be closer to the bar, so it made sense to stay and I found out later it was my grandfather who had coined the name Arsehola. Manning was full of noise and dust and unruly beer-soaked oilriggers during the early fifties. The bar was a constant source of aggravation to most of the wives of the patrons and mixed drinking was not allowed, so when a man finally wandered out drunk from his segregated swilling station to meet his wife, exiting from her own suds-salon, it was a clash of two solitudes. The overwhelming majority of the womenfolk wouldn't be caught dead in the bar and for a long time I thought a slut was a woman who drank beer.

In contrast North Star was an oasis of quiet. Nothing had happened since the majority had packed up and left to go to Manning for a permanent hangover. My dad looked after the Credit Union in North Star which was open on Saturdays. I would go along and visit the Nords on the farm, a portion of which had been donated by Oscar Nord to establish the village. The Credit Union was a shack on skids. It didn't look very stable and I always wondered why Dad was worried about getting collateral on a loan when the whole frigging lending institution could be hauled away by a Farmall tractor.

Sometimes I would sit in the sole remaining cafe which was run by Bill the Greek. I would listen to Bud Neal talking to his best friend, Andy Carmichael. Both of them would suck at their teeth before saying anything and then would use that sucking sound as punctuation. (Pursing of lips, inward sucking, squeaking sound) and then Bud would say, "Hot enough for you? Hot enough for you?" Andy would ponder for a heartbeat or so and the reply would come, "Just right. Just right." Then each would slurp at his coffee, pull out a cigarette, which they called "coffin nails," light it, take a couple of drags and, I swear, they always coughed in unison. "Gotta quit. Gotta quit." "Me too. Me too." The entire conversation would proceed like this day by day and year by year. The beauty of it was if you were eavesdropping and a bit hard of hearing you had a second shot at it. The other advantage was nobody ever had to say, "You can say that again."

Nobody can remember for sure how the whole thing got started. One night, in the middle of winter, an itinerant stuccoer-cum-carpenter, decided he had been filled with a healing power from the Lord. By word-of-mouth the good news spread and a couple of dozen curious folk assembled in the community hall at North Star. The Healer ranted and raved and shouted and writhed about on the stage. Come collection time the hat was filled with tens and twenties and even one beautiful fifty. The following night there was a huge crowd and I went along with my father to see the show. This fellow got up on the stage and hollered and jumped around and then asked for the deaf, the lame and the sick to come forward. He placed his hands on their afflicted parts and hollered. "Hush-a-ma-la kazoo. Huddica-huddica-ha." Some supplicants threw away their crutches and fell down. The ones who were deaf communicated by sign language to tell their loved ones they could hear and those with internal ailments felt better at once. The religious revival continued for weeks and I would sneak into the back of the hall and watch the Healer work his magic.

At home, I was trying to teach my dog Pal to heel, so I would put my hands on his head and say, "Hush-a-ma-la kazoo. Huddica-huddica-ha." Pal, who may have had a drop or two of Irish Setter in him and was therefore inevitably dumber than a bag of doorknobs, would run off to chase chickens.

The money kept pouring in to the Healer. The odd person died after being treated, but that was explained away on the grounds he didn't believe hard enough. Since the local doctor was already swamped with work, he wasn't about to complain about the competition. The Healer got so busy he turned down carpentry jobs and began to make plans to branch out into other communities like Hotchkiss and Deadwood. His last night in North Star, the whole crowd had been whipped into a froth and miracles were occurring at a dizzying pace. Diabetes was cured on the spot, cataracts dropped off, pimples dried up and ulcers were instantly vulcanized by the Healer's touch. Unfortunately, it was too much for one fellow who rose up from his seat on the backrow bench and ran towards the stage screaming. The Healer thought it was an ordinary patient who was a touch impatient and opened his arms to embrace another of his flock. The Healer was about half-way through his first Huddica, when the chap punched him square in the chops and turned his lights out for the rest of the evening. The RCMP constable was called and the attacker was taken away and sent out the next day to a mental hospital in Edmonton. Apparently, as a child, the fellow had seen a faith healer purport to heal his mother, but the treatment didn't take and she died. It was too much for him to see the fraud being born again and he snapped. It was also too much for the Healer and he drifted away for a few months.

When summer came and he drove back into North Star, a few locals joined him in Bill the Greek's cafe for a coffee. Someone asked him whether he was still preaching and the Healer allowed as he was back into carpentering and was looking for work. Either Andy or Bud asked him, "Howso? Howso?" And the Healer, with a straight, sober, almost beatific countenance, looked over the group and said, almost regretfully, "Jesus was a carpenter, too." Nobody could argue with that. So the Healer finished his coffee and took off in his beatup truck, tools rattling around in the back. The next time he was spotted, he was being chased down the road by an unsatisfied customer for totally buggering up a roof repair on a chicken coop.

About two months after the Healer was gone, Jake, a local farmer, got religion. He went away for a weekend to a seminary of sorts and came back a fully ordained Reverend. Since no one ever saw the certificate, it was suspected he had been practicing self-ordination, which, as opposed to self-abuse or self- flagellation, didn't cause blindness or leave scars. I went to the local church once to hear Jake preach and I liked his style.

We belonged to the United Church and their prayers never did take into account broad categories, so that at Thanksgiving, instead of thanking the Lord for a good harvest, the minister would begin to do a roll call of the different crops and varieties of vegetables. Once during the heavy-duty Thanksgiving prayer he accidentally read from his wife's grocery shopping list and had she not run short of canned fruit and "horsecock" we'd have never tumbled to it. Jake, however, was a man of few words and in his prayer of thanks said, "Lord, with that rain in July, we done pretty good." Some people came forward and confessed sins and Jake told the congregation he "used to drink now and then," which wasn't news but needed to be said. About two weeks later somebody found Jake out behind the hall during a wedding dance, lying on the ground in a fetal position, puking up that premixed lemon gin. He was forgiven but never preached again.

In retrospect Jake never promised anything and was an honest man who wasn't cut out to do the Lord's work in that way. It was rumoured during his evangelic career he took in only $13.68 in donations and accounted for every last cent.

I thought the local evangelical church was great. I can't remember the exact denomination but it wasn't Holy Rollers or people who spoke in tongues. It was more like Baptists who didn't have access to a drycleaner, so they stayed pretty well upright during the services. I was about six years old and was invited by the Reverend to come to something that night which he called "slides." I had no idea what that meant but went home and told my mother I was going tobogganing with the Reverend and she dressed me up in the usual twenty-seven layers of clothing and I dragged my toboggan to the church and left it outside. For about two hours we watched the Reverend stick pieces of cloth up on a board and then he hauled out what one person said was a "magic lantern," and Jesus and sheep and a lot of other stuff came up on a screen. Afterwards, we had cocoa and I pulled my toboggan home and Mom complimented me for not getting my clothes all wet like I usually did. I told her the religious people were very careful when they had slides, not like the Lovlin boys who would slide down a hill and hit the only tree within a mile.

I suppose North Star, like any other place, had people who went through bouts of good luck and disaster and hard times and some which weren't half-bad. Of course, there is always the extreme. There was a fellow called Cymbalik. Either the poor bugger never had a first name or if he did, no one used it or couldn't remember what it was. He was born, lived and then died in a mental home. A summary of his life appears at page 133 in the book, *Saga of Battle River*, as follows:

> Cymbalik filed on SW 5-93-23-W5 but never proved it.
> He built a barn and house all in one.
> He died in Oliver.

Proving once again that life is a series of shabby tricks.

# An Honest to God Western Producer
## Hal C. Sisson

At birth, to be sure that the child is breathing, a doctor has to take some action to make it cry. In Canada, if physical action doesn't cause crying, the doctor then tells the newborn baby it already owes $23,000...

At the other end of the spectrum, a doctor tells a patient he has only three months to live. "What shall I do?" asks the patient. "Well," says the doc, "I'd recommend three things — marry a nagging woman, get a job with McDonald's, and move to Winnipeg." "What good will that do?" queries the patient. "Nothing, but it will be the longest three months you ever spent!"

In between birth and death you have to make a living in this world, not only to supply your own food and small beer, but to help the government pay off the national debt. When I was born there was no national debt. There wasn't one even when my children were born, but my grandchildren owe a lot of money. There is no use bitching — we elected the people who made that possible. Retroactive birth control for all members of parliament is the only solution that would get us out of most of our Canadian problems.

So one does many things, takes many jobs, in the attempt to live in the style to which one would like to become accustomed. Most are eminently forgettable, but the odd one deserves recall.

When I was nineteen, I was frontman for a kidsnapper for a few summer months. That's the guy who travels door to door in advance of the photographer who takes children's pictures. You do the selling on a percentage basis and set up the appointments for the kidsnapper to attend at the household and take the pictures of the rug rats.

I spent four years in the Canadian Armed Forces, then five years at the University of Saskatchewan getting a law degree. Thousands of morons had passed the bar exam and I figured there was no reason I couldn't do the same. As a result of this ambition, I was usually semi-self-employed in the summers. Most jobs were interim, short term, selling something.

One summer job was selling beer — as a beerslinger at the Sylvan Lake Hotel and later at the Cascade Hotel in downtown Banff. In those days, Sylvan Lake was aptly called "the Tail of Two Cities," because of its location midway between Edmonton and Calgary. May as well have called Banff the tail of sixteen cities.

Both those hotels were tied to Calgary Brewing and, of course, all the draft that we flogged, twenty to a tray, was a Calgary Brewing Company product. One summer's afternoon, J.B. Cross came down into the Cascade Beer Parlour to sample a couple of his own brews. Fellow slinger Toss Stewart and I figured that J.B. should really be buying a round for the house. After all, he owned the joint. The Cascade sat about a thousand people on a Saturday night, but on a weekday afternoon a round wouldn't cost much — might be only thirty or forty people there and beer was ten cents a glass.

Toss and I decided to try and show J.B. up, by buying several rounds for the house ourselves. Plaudits from the regular drinking customers, but no reaction whatsoever from the Calgary Brewing magnate who never did buy a round. Drank a few of our drafts and left. Guess that is the best way to accumulate a fortune — don't blow money on booze.

Some reward was reaped however. We were off shift at 4:00 PM and sat down for a couple of beers ourselves. Couldn't pay for a damn thing all evening. Beer just kept arriving at our table from many directions. The afternoon customers who stayed on had likely never encountered waiters who provided free beer, and were willing to reciprocate. I had too many over the eight that evening.

We had been relieved by the evening shift of beer slingers, one of whom was Hughie Cawker of Winnipeg, as well developed a man as I have ever seen. Sitting at a table having a beer, he would decide it was time to go to the can. Hughie would stand up, do a hand stand and walk on his hands for twenty yards, up several steps, down a hall and into the men's lavatory. Still on his hands he would approach the urinal, relieve himself from this upside down position, zip up again, and hand walk all the way back to his table. Try it sometime!

Hughie was a veteran whose English war-bride had been killed in an air raid, and for awhile after WWII he just wandered the globe as a nomad. After Banff he joined the French Foreign Legion and had one arm blown off at Dienbienphu. Too bad — he would thereafter have to go to the pissoire standing up like the rest of us.

I sold other things like life insurance and the *Books of Knowledge* for the Grolier Society. Cold turkey selling is not for everyone — door-to-door, farmhouse-to-farmhouse — it was and is a tough way to make a living. Unless and until you become good at it — then the remuneration can be very satisfactory. Nowadays not many of those kinds of jobs exist; most things are sold by TV and credit cards from Box 500, Toronto or some other big city.

For instance I don't see or hear of any sheetwriters of late. I did that job one summer for a news agency out of Saskatoon, who handled the Wheat Pool farmer's weekly newspaper, *The Western Producer*. The agency also handled various magazines, but by far the easiest thing to sell was the *Producer*, and it made the salesman a much larger commission. So we flogged it with a vengeance through every hamlet and farm in Saskatchewan and Alberta in the summer of 1948. I think the reason we didn't go into Manitoba was that it was too near the home of the *Producer*'s main farm-paper rival, the *Winnipeg Free Press*. The basic subscription rate was $3 a year. A good buy because, even if the purchasing household didn't read it in the outhouse, there was plenty of paper left over to start the stove in the morning. Two years were five bucks, three years for seven and so on. Out of every dollar the salesman got seventy cents, the crew boss got an override of another ten cents, the news agency got fifteen cents, and *The Western Producer* got one big solitary nickel.

The biggest problem arose every Monday morning. Trying to get your ass in gear and forcing yourself out into the territory you had chosen to work that week. So you really didn't get going well until Tuesday, and by Thursday night the whole crew had started to think how nice it would be to go into Sylvan Lake or Regina Beach for a weekend party. But in mid-week it was an interesting job, talking to a great many people while testing your nerve and selling skills. Furthermore, pay day was immediate and always in cash.

To be successful, you had to make people feel at ease while spending a modicum of time on the call. Many were already getting the *Producer*. You could tell when the subscription ran out by the code printed under their name on the front page. So what to do when you had found a satisfied reader and he was already signed up for three years? Well, you told him the story — in fact, you told it anyway, no matter how long his subscription ran and especially if he wasn't taking the paper at all. The spiel went like this:

"Sir, do you take the *Toronto Star Weekly*?"
"Yes."
"Do you and the family, the kids, like the coloured comics in that weekly paper?"
"Sure do!"
"And you know it is printed down East, in Toronto?"
"Of course."
"Did you ever wonder why our own Western Prairie paper doesn't have a comic section, can't afford it in fact?"
"Well, I never gave it much thought, but it would be nice if they did have the comics."
"Would you like to help them get a comic section?"
"Certainly, if I could. But how would I do that?"
"The reason those damned blood-sucking Easterners can do it, is that they siphon off all the advertising money down to Toronto. Ain't enough of it left for us Westerners. And you're going to ask me how they do that. Well, they do it through a guaranteed subscription list that is big enough to attract the large advertisers who want to be sure they sell their products."
"Is that so?"
"Sure is. That's how papers make their money. Through the advertisers, not through the very small subscription fee that we are offering to you today. But the advertisers won't spend their money unless the paper has a large number of signed-up readers like you."
"Sounds right, but I am signed up with the *Producer*."
"I know, but not for long enough to get you coloured comics. *The Western Producer* has figured out what it will take to attract the big advertisers, what they need in order to make comics a break-even proposition before supplying them to their readers. They figure that they have to have one hundred thousand readers signed up for ten years — and if they can do that then they can afford to give the West their own coloured comic section. And another thing, important to remember, is that they can then prevent all that advertising money from going down East to those damned Torontonians."

"Oh, that would be a good thing," says the farmer. "We don't want all that money going down East. They don't deserve it. Why, I remember the days when we was close to starvin' out here in the Depression, and we never got a damned thing from the East, except maybe a few frozen cod from the herring chokers. Christ, they was so hard and dried out you could have used them to shingle your roof."

And then you really had to try and stop the vituperative diatribe that the farmer started to unload on those poor unsuspecting Eastern bastards. They didn't even know they were being maligned, but they sure as hell were helping us sell a lot of *The Western Producer* in Eyebrow, Saskatchewan and Manyberries, Alberta. Most of the time you could get the three-year subscriber to sign up for ten, and most others for some increase in the number of years they were already taking the paper. To my knowledge *The Western Producer* never did print a coloured comic section. Maybe they are still one short of the hundred thousand subscribers at ten years each. However, that was our idea of how they should operate and if they didn't want to take our advice, they didn't have to. We were just trying to help out our own and the western economy by trading on the traditional animosity and rivalry that existed between the have and have-not regions of Canada. Still does.

We traveled in two cars, usually — six people, three men and two women, all university students, and the crew boss Norm. On one occasion, we pulled into this village from one direction and a female crew of four women sheetwriters, from the Golightly agency in Winnipeg, pulled in from the other. Ten door-to-door salesmen at once in a place that likely didn't constitute more that twenty calls. Butts were hustling in every direction and some people must have been hit four or five times before we figured out what was happening. Everyone ended up in the beer parlour where we drank lunch.

Then there was the time our crew hit Wilkie, Saskatchewan one afternoon and found hundreds of parked cars around and about the Town Community Centre. Naturally, we went in. It turned out to be a meeting of Wheat Pool members discussing farm problems. We couldn't really sell because the meeting was in progress, but we tried around the fringes and with farmers outside having a smoke. This could be a bonanza but how to get to as many as possible or even get to anybody before the meeting broke up and they dispersed. Information from a couple of farmers we did talk to was to the effect that one of the items on the meeting's agenda was *The Western Producer* farm paper, and how maybe farmers could help the paper financially by dealing directly with the newspaper office when subscribing. This was sacrilege to our ears — anathema. What could we do to prevent this double impasse — how to get to make a pitch at all, and how to prevent them from buying elsewhere.

We took the crew boss over in the corner and talked to him hard. "Look, Norm old boy, you gotta do something here. This is your big chance to earn that ten percent override you get from us for doing sweet bugger all. Now, talk to the chairman, and then get up on that stage and give them The Spiel! The coloured comic section, the goddamn Torontonians, the whole bit."

I'll hand it to Norm. Well-dressed, soft-spoken but forceful, he rabble-roused those farmers in fine fashion, told them how his whole family had been foreclosed and run off the land by Eastern bankers, how he had to sell blood to the Red Cross once a month to put bread on the table for his kids, and how now that he had got this job he was determined to get the subscribers and the advertisers so that the faithful readers of *The Western Producer* could read coloured comics every week. He inspired their trust by offering to help with their problems. He tried for their pity by telling them that his crew of students, working their way through college, some of them veterans, were present and ready to take their subscriptions. It was good stuff, brought tears to my eyes. After Norm was through speaking, we must have hit for a hundred bucks each on the afternoon's work.

Good money in Wilkie in 1948, and we did our bit for the good old *Western Producer* — the average time of a subscription was lengthened and the paper must have made at least twenty bucks for themselves, thus refuting the adage that if you throw your bread upon the waters it will always come back soggy and unfit to eat.

# The Luck of the Draw

Dwayne W. Rowe

Although the curling rink opened up to allow womenfolk to participate, there was still a ban on kids playing the "roaring game." We used to go down to the rink and sit on those hard wooden benches in the waiting room to watch our fathers curl. One had to be very lucky to be allowed out on the ice after everyone had left to throw a couple of practice rocks down one sheet, while Art Pierce, the ice-maker, was cleaning up.

In those days there was no such thing as matched rocks. Everyone bought their own set and were damned lucky if the two of them matched, let alone looked like the stones belonged to someone else. Some were flatter than others, some were higher and some had a funny mottled colour. In order to distinguish the rocks of one team from the other, the side losing the coin toss had to put red tassels around the handles. Since the rocks of the lead on Team A and the rocks of the third on Team B came from the same supplier and were identical, the tassel was extremely important. One of the rocks would pull more than the other, therefore the curler would have his own secret designation permitting him to identify the one with the aberrant penchant for hooking to the left at the dying moment, just as it was about to enter the twelve-foot circle.

My father's rocks were flatter than most and seemed to be rounder which caused a few arguments when deciding whether or not he had a "biter." One fellow had rocks so high they looked like jam cans and would actually teeter as they went down the sheet. The ice was natural and, at forty below, the pebble was a combination of the hot water droplets sprayed by Art Pierce from the weird contraption he had slung over his back and the tendency for a half inch of frost to collect on the surface. As a result it was often a contest of strength just to heave a rock from the hack to the other end.

This was the reason I was told I could not curl with my father's team in the Men's League until I weighed one hundred and twenty pounds. It seemed that no matter what I ate I could not hit that goal. I kept on growing until my legs were up under my chin. I looked like a clothespin. One October day, after the Big Freeze, I stuffed my pockets with rocks, fiddled with the adjustment on the scale, waited until my father had finished a bottle of whiskey with his friend and then had him watch as I weighed myself. It is difficult to bend down to read the numbers at the best of times and as he slipped and fell to the floor I said, "One twenty — on the nose." As he was not in the mood for a recount, the figure was taken as the truth. I started out playing lead and was indeed a natural at it. I got the turns right and would throw a "dead-handle" now and then, but knew an "out" from an "in" and was pretty good at hitting the broom.

Art Pierce, who was legally blind, played second for us sometimes. In order that Art see the broom, Dad, who was skipping, would wave it back and forth like a pendulum. Art would catch the motion and then could follow it as it was placed on the ice.

Before the first season was over I had graduated to playing third. We came in second in the annual bonspiel, losing out in the Grand Challenge Event by one rock on the tenth end. We won TV trays as our prize, while the winners got Hudson Bay blankets. The TV trays and their complex tripod design fascinated guests for years to come, but by the time the Manning area actually got TV reception fifteen years later the trays were considered to be tacky. Then fifteen years after that were considered to be art deco and worth a fortune.

Watching curling on television nowadays is a bit like watching fruit ripen, even with the new changes in the rules designed to speed up the game and keep some rocks in play. The knockout game was frowned upon back then and most times about twelve rocks would be in the house. If a spring thaw happened to arrive mid-way through the game, a rock would push water ahead of it as it entered the house, plow to a stop and then stick there to the rings. Unless it was knocked out in the next couple of shots, it would settle into the ice until it couldn't be dislodged even with an express-train zinger of a throw. The targeted rock would take the hit, bounce up an inch or so and settle back into the hole. More than a few eight-enders were counted in the course of a season and six was not uncommon.

There was no such thing as a shotclock or timer back in those days. If someone known to be agonizingly slow didn't take a few friendly hints to speed up his delivery, someone from his own team or an opponent would walk back to the hack and crack him over the head with a broom. It seemed to correct the problem and is an example of behaviour conforming to expectations, much like men washing their hands after using the urinal provided someone else is in the can at the same time. (A classic example of pee-er pressure.)

The amount of debris on the ice from the old straw brooms was sometimes enough to make a fairly decent bundle if one had taken the time to run a binder down the ice. There were three sheets of ice and the middle one was the truest. A spectator walkway ran down between that sheet and number three which tended to have a slope at the far end where the scoreboard hung. Depending on the ice conditions a skip on Sheet Three would have to excuse himself and intrude on the house on Sheet Two in order to put down the broom and allow the shooter enough leeway to take advantage of the fall in the ice. Now and then some out-of-town salesmen would be sitting in the gallery watching a game. They would be astounded at the ability of a lead to hit the broom dead on in the middle of Sheet Two and draw to the button directly ahead of him. The protocol was to ask the skip on Sheet Two to borrow his spot. Only once did I see a breach of this etiquette lead to a fist fight. The local RCMP Corporal, who was sitting in the gallery, intended to intervene but the sight of elderly curlers punching each other as the entire complement of four teams became involved was too much for him and he just lay down on the bench and roared. Pretty soon the curlers on the other sheets started to laugh and, after a couple of last minute punches, the donnybrook was over. The guys were so embarrassed they just kicked the rocks out of the house without counting the end and called it a blank. It was an interesting display of human behaviour — to see the opposing teams join forces to battle the intruders from the other sheet, putting aside their erstwhile rivalry in defence of territorial integrity.

The highlights of the season were the club playdowns to see which team would go to the North Peace Championship, and the local bonspiel. Due to the interest shown, the bonspiel ran on a round-the-clock basis. If one team was winning in two events at the same time, they played practically non-stop until they lost or were admitted to hospital for hypothermia, blisters, backpain or alcohol poisoning. A lot of drinking went on during a bonspiel and even people who didn't drink all year would get pie-eyed at the 'spiel. An unwritten rule was that no more than two members of the team could get drunk at a time so there were always two semi-sober members to pick up the slack. Since two of the opposing team were also drunk there was a level playing field (except on Sheet Three, of course).

One time, at a 4:00 AM draw, an otherwise brilliant shot maker had problems with his weight and consistently drew the front hog-line, which cut down on the sweeping required, a fact appreciated by his teammates. In those days the scoring was done by hanging little metal plates over the numbers; this scoring system was tricky to read at the best of times. If a plate with the number 1 was hanging over the painted number 4 on the board, that meant the team with the red tassels on their rocks scored four on the first end. The difficulty lay in trying to hang the little numbered plates over the nails protruding from the board. With a bit of the grape circulating in the system at four o'clock in the morning it sometimes proved to be so troublesome that one of the curlers would keep score by writing it down on his cigarette pack. This drove the spectators to fits as they never knew for sure who was winning.

Out-of-town teams stayed in the local hotel and the idea was for the locals to feed them so much booze they would sleep in and have to forfeit the game, or at least a couple of points, for showing up late. One visiting team had a designated waker-upper and after three consecutive 4:00 AM draws (the drawmaster was a local) he was finally getting some rest about noon when the fire siren went off. He got out of bed, got dressed, picked up his broom and walked directly into the wall, breaking his glasses and nose in that order.

You could always tell the smart-alecks from out of town as they tended to slide when they delivered the rock, something learned in the big city where they had artificial iceplants in the rinks. The locals slid out on one knee, balancing stork-like until the rock could be released. After about four games back-to-back, the kneecap started to develop the kind of sensitivity usually associated with carbuncles and hemorrhoids — so a variety of ingenious devices were invented to soften the impact. Some wore two extra pairs of longjohns which made a suitable cushion for the knees but when it came time to run to the bathroom between sweeping assignments, it was a matter of fumbling with three fly-openings or three trapdoors in the back of the underwear; no mean feat in an outdoor toilet while wearing gloves. A couple of people tried hockey pads under their pants but they were hard and slippery and could cause a person to slide out crooked, like a ship with a busted rudder. The usual footwear was either moccasins with a rubber on one foot or overshoes with five flaps, not a composition by Mozart, but oversize boots with a complicated system of buckles. Usually the buckling apparatus was left to flap open on both shoes, which could lead to a sudden catching of the parts causing both feet to tie up suddenly while the body continued to move forward, face-down on the ice.

One year a young chap had been keeping company with a gal who had a bit of trouble keeping track of events according to the calendar. This error led to their sudden marriage. Unfortunately, the nuptials took place on the first day of the annual bonspiel. The young man was not only a winner in the game of matrimony but his team also got hot. They were winning all their games in both the A and the B event, which meant they were playing about five games a day. Between games poor Charlie would grab a bite to eat and run back to the motel to visit his bride. About halfway through his third game on the last day of the spiel, as they were playing for the Grand Challenge Trophy, he fell asleep in the hack, sitting bolt upright, his glazed eyes staring at the far end of the rink. His skip wanted him to come down with nice draw weight and tap up one of his own rocks about four feet which would put it neatly in the twelve-foot ring.

"Charlie," the skip yelled, "can you raise one?"

Charlie woke up with a start and said, "Jeez, honey, give me a break, I gotta curl in an hour."

They eventually won the game and the trophy and he

dragged himself back to the motel, looking like he'd been pulled through a knothole backwards. Big Jake, who was a confirmed bachelor, watched him leave and offered up the comment, "My hands may be sore, but I sure wouldn't wanta trade blisters with that boy."

The game of curling has undergone changes — some for the better and some not. Experimentation and variation is an inherent facet of the sport much like chess or flycasting. In all of these endeavours one can be taught the basics in about twenty minutes and then spend three lifetimes getting better at it. In curling, it is more than calling the shots, hitting the broom, getting the weight just so, reading the ice, sweeping smartly, keeping up morale, strategizing and out-thinking the opponent. It is an exercise in combat, a participation in comprehending the subtle application of the fields of force. Hockey players and commentators talk about momentum, but, like baseball and life generally, in curling things can go to hell in an instant. No matter how carefully constructed the house, no matter how well placed the guards, no matter how sweetly put the shot-rock, if you were playing against Johnny Tanne, you were on the edge of disaster. Johnny could slip in the hack, throw the wrong turn, pick up a straw, bang into a guard, drive it through a tiny port, wick off the number four shot-rock and end up knocking out the winning stone. Then he would dance up and down and cackle and chortle and giggle while grown men on the opposing team alternately wept or dreamed of shoving a broom up Johnny's fundamental orifice.

"How does that man walk," they would wonder over coffee later, "with those horseshoes up his ass?" The fact is the losers had faced someone with karma, someone in whose little body the forces of yin and yang were in balance and the five elements in harmony. Why fight it? In one bonspiel Johnny had fluked about four more wild ones than was usual even for him. We were tied up going home and he had last rock. I had one of my boys bury one so far back in the house you couldn't have hit it with a slingshot, and threw a pile of garbage out front. Sitting in the other hack you would have needed a periscope to see the red tassel on our winning stone. Johnny went down to shoot and I told my team we were done for.

"If he makes that shot," said Ray, "I'll cut my broom into pieces and eat the sonofabitch like shredded wheat." Johnny squatted down, let the rock loose. It was about four feet off the broom with the wrong turn. It had good speed on it, though, and caught a fall in the ice, hooked to the right, slid through a port, still running at a pretty good clip and then veered to the left and ground to a sudden halt. It was close enough we had to measure, but he had us by about an inch. When we lifted up the rock we found part of an Export A cigarette butt sticking to the bottom. We all knew who smoked that brand and, as Johnny lit one up, he shook our hands and said, "Good game, boys, for a minute there I thought I was going to miss that one."

Ray said the broom lasted pretty well through spring and wasn't half bad if he sprinkled brown sugar on it and added a cup of boiling water. In fact it was serendipitous as the high fibre content eaten by him that winter has stood him in good stead throughout the years and regularity is still one of the things he can count on even now at age fifty-three.

The sport of curling is a great leveller. There is no social structure which is permitted to impede. If you like curling and put your heart into it and are a good guy, then that is the end of it. And the best of all was that women were allowed to be good guys and share in a true fellowship, uncomplicated by a bunch of expensive consultants gazing into their navels and coming out with a bunch of crap which one way or the other offends one of the only two officially recognized sexes. In the smaller centres all over the prairies, the annual ritual of bonspiels was pretty much the same.

For example, during a bonspiel in Springwater, Saskatchewan, the well-to-do drank port from gallon jugs which were stored in the pumphouse room at the rink. One of the initiation rites for a novice but up-and-coming curler was to be invited by the icemaker into the pumphouse for a healthy swig of "Pumphouse Port." One grasped the handle, threw the jug up on one shoulder and glugged down three or four swallows.

Some curlers had their own alcoholic beverage and drank it from Mason jars right out on the ice. The police could always tell when a Springwater guy had been drinking at a 'spiel from looking at the ring on his nose left by the Mason jar. It was a dead giveaway, much like a housewife trying to convince her hubby coming home from work that she had had a busy day keeping house, which is a tough sell, especially when she didn't have the foresight to erase the Chenille marks from her face.

One of the toughest assignments in sport is to remain cool under pressure. The great ones all have that ability, like Al "The Iceman" Hackner or Ed Werenich or the brilliant shotmaker Hec Gervais. For a skip sitting alone in that hack staring at a wide-open take-out, which can win the whole megillah, it requires total concentration, a slowing down of the heartbeat, consummate breath control and the ability to focus energy on the target. This is tough to do at the best of times, but in Springwater it was even tougher, the reason being that if you were playing against Jenny McMillan and happened to win the game then instead of shaking hands she would beat you with her broom. Apart from personal experience felt by some, the word got around that the final shot against Jenny could bring either the agony of victory or the comfort of defeat. Did The Iceman or Hec every sit in the hack at the World Championships knowing that their steely determination in pulling off the shot would inevitably lead to Lars Lundquist of Sweden pounding the hell out of them with one of those wooden pushbrooms?

Curling involves the law of physics. A practical demonstration was held at the rink in Springwater when Pooper Martin threw a rock as hard as he could from one hack while another fellow threw one just as hard from the opposite end. The rocks collided in the middle of the sheet, dead on, and broke in half. Now there were eighteen rocks to play with instead of sixteen but two of them didn't have a handle. The conclusion drawn by the spectators was if two powerfully built farmboys throw a real "beaner" — that is, a curling rock with the velocity of a bullet and they collide and bust into pieces, then granite ain't what it is cracked up to be.

Even in those days curling could become an obsession. There were no cash 'spiels or big prizes other than the Nipawin car bonspiel in Saskatchewan. Dedication to the sport interfered with work. For Willy Hooper, curling was an avocation, a mission, and he was one of the best shotmakers around. One day he was leaving work in the middle of the afternoon with his curling broom and shoes over his shoulder when the boss said to him, snarly-like, "One of these days you're going to have to make up your mind whether you want to work here or curl."

Willy turned around, looked at the man and said, "I don't know why you're still confused — there's no doubt in my mind," and left for the rink. Willy was such a good salesman and did so well from his contacts at the curling club that he always managed to survive the guillotine. When he told us the query his boss had put to him, we were also astounded and realized the ignorant will always be with us. Explaining curling to a man like that is like trying to convince some long-haired, weirdo, hippie music professor that Kitty Wells didn't have a sinus condition. It isn't worth the trouble.

Many years later in a lawyer's curling bonspiel in Edmonton, Harry the Pick, was out on the ice with a mickey of Scotch in his back pocket. He was running alongside a real "beaner" trying to sweep a clear path in front when he fell on his butt. The bottle broke and when he got up it was obvious medical attention was required. He was driven to the hospital lying face down in the back of a car. At the hospital emergency room his buddies filled out the appropriate forms explaining the nature of the problem.

As luck would have it, one of the trauma surgeons on duty was an avid curler, as was his chief nurse. A couple of other doctors happened by and they divided into two teams for the purpose of picking the tiny shards from Harry's quivering buttocks. The job required a considerable amount of dexterity. The medical professionals not only took pride in their work, they were naturally competitive in nature. A few weeks later word got out that in one doctor's office there was a plaque on the wall that read:

*Winner*
*For picking glass*
*from the Ass of Harry the Pick*
*Closest to the Button*

# High Prairie Hat Trick

Hal C. Sisson

It was thirty degrees below zero when Pop Polski parked his 1937 red Chevy truck in front of the High Prairie General Mercantile Store belonging to his young relative, Sid Kovnats. The snow had stopped falling, but the temperature had started dropping. And the temperature was none of this Celsius you get nowadays, but honest to God Fahrenheit stuff — real cold, with no added wind chill factor to confuse the issue.

Winter's early night had fallen in the late afternoon when Pop had dropped off his load of raw fur at the S. Slutker & Co. warehouse. Several hundred dollars worth, in fact, as he'd had a good trip along Lesser Slave Lake dealing with Indian trappers. Due to the cold he left the motor running in the old truck, with keys in the ignition. Shut her down and you may not get her started again too easy in this weather.

When his step-dad entered the emporium, Sid Kovnats was at the cash register, gassing with Ruby Wong who ran the greasy spoon next door. Pop Polski joined in the conversation.

"You guys know why sex is like a snowstorm?" Ruby was asking.

"No, but I'm sure you're going to tell us," said Sid.

"Well, you never know how long it's going to last or how many inches you're going to get!" Laughter all around as Sid replied to the departing Ruby, "Your break-away panties will be in next week."

The Mercantile carried everything — everything that the management could either get on consignment or afford to buy. But times were hard and when stock was low Sid had to make it look bigger. So he specialized in Kellogg's Corn Flakes, always getting the largest size so it would take up more shelf space. Half the store was sometimes covered with Corn Flakes. He also traded in cattle, pigs and fur — anything to make a buck.

The store needed help. It was Friday night, near supper time, and the place was busy. "Pop, can you stick around and lend me a hand for a while?" asked Sid. "I'm really short-handed."

"Yeah, I guess so," said Pop. "It ain't like I'm doing anything else, and maybe I can get some supper out of you later on."

"We could tie on the feedbag at the hotel when we close up, but no steaks — we ain't that busy." But they were and half an hour passed quickly before Pop, who was behind the till, yelled at Sid, "Hey, I forgot to turn off my motor — the truck will get too damn hot, overheat — run out like a good boy and turn the heap off, will you?"

Sid, who was near the door, didn't exactly leap into action, but he knew that cars had to be coddled in such cold weather — keep them warm but don't overdo it. He went out into the high street and looked for his father's truck, which he rightfully expected would be somewhere in the immediate vicinity, chugging away in the arctic air. There were several cars doing just that, but no beat-up red Chevy truck to be seen. He came in out of the cold blowing on his hands. "Where did you park it, Pop, down around Enilda?"

"You schlemiel, it's right outside near the street lamp. You blind or don't you recognize it?"

Sid went outside again. No truck. He went down as far as the cafe and looked up the alley. His dad could have parked it there and forgotten. No jalopy. He went back into the store and remonstrated with Pop.

"What are you, some kind of dibbic? It's right out there, I tell you — I'll do it myself." And Pop came around the counter and went out the door into the cold night.

Only to return thirty seconds later in a state of frenetic excitement. "The sonofabitch is gone! What in tarnation — it's gone. GONE!" Pop was shouting and everyone in the store heard him and started to gather at the front counter.

"You mean —?"

"They've stolen my goddamn truck!"

Sid and Pop ran out into the snow-blown street again, several customers following them. "It was parked right here," said Pop, pointing to the spot. "Goddamn crooks — can't leave nothin' alone. Those rotten bastards." Pop started to kick the telephone pole that carried the street light under which he had parked his vehicle. This only hurt his foot and he limped back into the general store along with the onlookers. Sid phoned the RCMP and reported the theft of an automobile.

The police automatically headed in the direction of the Atikameg Indian Reserve as soon as they got the report that the truck was missing. High Prairie might be the murder capital of Canada, but there were no big-time car thieves operating in the area. It figured to be a local drunk trying to get home before he sobered up or froze to death.

Winter roads in the area were bad — especially the side roads. A person would ask, "How's the road to so-and-so place?" And local people would either reply, "Don't ask!" or they would say, "Well, Pop Polski was over it a couple of days ago, so it should be fair." They would also ask if the Alberta government grader had plowed out the road recently. If so, then you'd better drive in the ditch, they'd say. At least in the ditch a person knew what conditions to expect.

So while Polski could drive a vehicle over or through anything, the same couldn't be said for whoever had purloined his truck, because the cops found it piled into a snow-filled ditch out past Wabasca, east of town. The truck was not damaged. Closer to the settlement of Wabasca, the red riders of the snow-laden green spruce, Sergeant Brown and Constable Nivens, also found one of the Mackenzie clan, wandering on and off the road and in and out of the ditch, and fast running out of enough gas in his gizzard to keep him mobile. They didn't catch him in the car — close but no cigar. And Mackenzie got himself a free musical ride back to High Prairie in the cop car, a ride he didn't want but which likely kept him from freezing to death.

Sergeant Harry Brown, who was in the business of helping people to repent, asked the weary traveler for his name.

"My name is...ah...ah...Dan!"

"Dan? Daniel, you say? What's your last name?"

"My name is...ah...ah...Dan!"

"I see. Dan Dan — that's a biblical name, my old son. Well, we'll see. Now it is my duty to inform you that you have the right to retain and instruct counsel without delay. Do you understand?"

"I...ah...ah...my name is Dan. I think...do...understan' what?"

It was like talking to a bedroll. "You understand that means you are being charged with car theft and that you have the right to call a lawyer."

Dan slumped back into the seat. The sergeant would have to wait and see, because Dan didn't tell Brown anything that would help the sergeant aid and abet Dan into confession or repentance of his alleged crime.

They took Dan Dan back to High Prairie Mercantile from whence Brown strongly suspected, in fact was sure, Dan had started his journey not too long ago in the stolen Chevy truck. They went into the warm store, linked together by handcuffs, and, Brown leading the way, marched up to Sid and the still irate Pop Polski.

"Know this joker, Sid?" asked Brown.

"Yes, he's a Mackenzie kid, I think," Sid replied, which wasn't only a guess on Sid's part. The name Mackenzie was longstanding and time-honoured in the Peace River country, ever since the days of Alexander, who had first overwintered there in 1793, the first white man to do so. Alex couldn't possibly have been the real grand-ancestor of all the hundreds of present-day Mackenzies in the Peace. He may have been a sex maniac, but history didn't think he could have passed the physical for such a prodigious task. A lot of Indian and Metis families took his famous name or else the fur companies just gave it to them for identity purposes.

Sid was familiar with the denizens of the reserves, the spruce outback, the deep bush. They came to the biggest town around, came regularly into his store for supplies.

"You see him in here today?" asked Brown.

"He was in the store earlier."

"How much earlier?"

"Like, I dunno, maybe I saw him wandering about in here late afternoon."

"Buy anything?"

"Nope. Where did you pick him up?"

"Wabasca, near there. Truck was in the ditch. It ain't hurt, Pop."

"Where'n hell's it at now?" asked Pop.

"It's still in the ditch. We're getting it brung in, don't sweat it. But we got to get a team of horses out there to extract it from the ditch, where somebody," and here Brown paused to look at Mackenzie with a cold eye, "who was a shitty driver, musta left it."

Dan wasn't saying anything. He had sobered up enough to start heeding the basic rules of survival. No *mea culpa* for him. Don't talk to the cops any more than you have to, you could get convicted out of your own mouth.

"Damn it, I need that truck to make a buying trip out to Winagami Lake," complained Pop, "or somebody'll beat me to that fur."

"Not my department, Pop. You'll get it back as soon as we get it back. Meanwhile I'm charging Dan Dan here with larceny!"

"Hope it ain't petty, my truck's a big item —better make it grand larceny!"

"It'll come under the proper section of the Criminal Code. And I'll need you down at the station to swear out a complaint. Take you down right now if you want, and get the constable here to drive you back."

And Pop got his vehicle back very late the next day, but he missed out on some fur which cheesed him off no end.

The trial was held up in the town of Peace River, just below the meeting of the Smoky and Peace rivers. The courtroom was in the meeting hall of the United Church, Judge Steven Worsthorne presiding. The judge was a lay magistrate appointed by the government of Premier Ernest Manning. The vast majority of the legal profession of the time wouldn't buy the funny money theories of the Social Credit as originally promulgated by Bible Bill Aberhart. So the attorney general's office (Manning was also the attorney general) appointed provincial lay magistrates from the ranks of loyal Social Credit Party businessmen in the community —never from the members of the legal profession. Worsthorne was the local pharmacist and owner of the drugstore —his legal decisions were all over like a dog's breakfast, usually favouring the prosecution, as why else would the cops have brought this criminal to trial if he wasn't guilty? However, you could never be quite sure, for the judge seldom made his decisions on any known legal precepts. He maddened a lot of people. One recipient of one of his judicial decisions expressed the desire to knock up his daughter just so Steve would have to walk the floor with his bawling kid.

This was the judge before whom our culprit's trial was

to be heard, but Dan Dan McKenzie had taken Sergeant Brown's standard perfunctory advice and retained and instructed none other than "Old Man" Baldwin, the dean emeritus and fastest mouthpiece of the legal profession in the North.

Brown had subpoenaed Sid and Pop for the trial. He had to, because when Sid found out the negligibility of the witness fees for appearing at trial in Peace River as a crown witness, he refused to go voluntarily. Hence the subpoena to ensure his presence! Sid likely would have reconsidered and done his duty — but the subpoena was a precautionary measure. No one should ask for justice unless they are prepared to accept both the court decision and the inconvenience involved in obtaining it.

When he learned that the car thief had hired legal counsel, Sergeant Brown increased his efforts to prepare his case well. To this end he secured the capable services of the Peace River Crown agent, Alexander "Sandy" Phimester. No worries there, although the RCMP at this time primarily conducted and prosecuted their own cases. Nowadays thousands of morons are graduating from law colleges, so that the government department of attorneys general have to hire a goodly number of them as Crown prosecutors — sort of a make-work project like Legal Aid, good for the economy in both good times and in recession; and of course the crime rate increases as the population rises.

The day of the trial dawned as it always must do. Sid and Pop, Sergeant Brown and Constable Nivens, Dan Mackenzie and a couple of car loads of Atikameg Indians, all drove the winter-wind and snow-blasted gravel highway from High Prairie to Peace River, a cold and gruesome eighty-six miles.

After the usual small court business and guilty pleas, Judge Worsthorne's court clerk called the main event of the day, Regina vs. Daniel Mackenzie. In one corner the Queen and her minions in scarlet uniform and black robe, in the other corner Dan Mackenzie in blue denim and Old Man Baldwin in a seersucker suit. (He was the sucker who had bought it from Sears.)

De rigueur, and, as usual, the prosecution was first to present their case to the court. After the opening statement by Sandy Phimester as to the bare bones and basic nature of the facts by which the Crown intended to prove the criminal Mackenzie guilty of car theft, Old Man Baldwin made a standard opening gambit – he asked for exclusion of witnesses and the trial was on. Baldwin didn't have any witnesses except for the accused, and he couldn't risk putting Dan Mackenzie on the stand, so exclusion of witnesses could only be to his advantage. This procedure is not unusual, and so Pop and Sid and Nivens had to wait out in the church proper, where they sat in the empty pews and contemplated the pulpit. Brown was the first Crown witness, so he stayed on in the courtroom and gave his testimony as to where he had found Pop's car and where he had found the accused Mackenzie – no other tracks and no evidence of the presence of anybody else – only circumstantial but highly incriminating.

Nivens, and then Pop, were called in next, leaving Sid all by his lonesome in the ecclesiastically foreign atmosphere of the United Church. He thought about getting up in the pulpit and rendering a sermon to an imaginary congregation. He'd take for his text a phrase in the Bible which he had always admired, "He gave her wine and nectar!"

What in blazes were they doing in there, what was taking them so long, he wondered. Also what questions would he be asked – but then he was only there to prove Mackenzie's presence in High Prairie shortly before his similar presence near the ditched truck in Wabasca. That would be a breeze.

The court attendant showed up, beckoned, and Sid was ushered into the courtroom, Lawyer Phimester requesting that he be sworn and take his place in the box.

The first thing Sid noticed were three hats lined up on the defence counsel's table, which was immediately facing the witness box. The prosecution led him through his evidence, and Old Man Baldwin didn't make any objections, as Sid identified the accused and allowed as how the Mackenzie youth had been in his mercantile store in High Prairie about a half hour prior to Pop's parking his truck and entering the premises. It didn't take long and Sid felt that he had given positive testimony. This would wrap up the case.

"Your witness, Mr. Baldwin," said Mr. Phimester and sat down behind his Sunday school table. Old Man Baldwin approached the witness stand. He knew Sid, he knew Pop, he'd shopped at the High Prairie Mercantile when his practice took him to that town.

"No need to ask you, Sid, but you'll answer my questions truthfully and to the best of your ability?"

"Certainly, Mr. Baldwin."

"You've been to Atikameg?"

"Yes, on occasion."

"Not a place anybody's likely to go unless it was his home?"

"No."

"Not too many of the amenities of life out there?"

"Hmmmm . . . no."

"Somebody said that if they were going to give Alberta an enema they'd insert the tube at Atikameg. Do you agree with that?"

"Is this relevant, Mr. Baldwin?" asked Worsthorne, trying the judging role on for size.

"Just a point of departure, Your Worship. Perhaps — to shorten or state the point — the people of Atikameg or Wabasca are not too flush with money or means of transportation — and if they wanted to get home badly enough, any number of the residents there might have taken a running motor vehicle into their own hands for the purpose?"

Sandy Phimester came to his feet in a hurry, "I object! My learned friend is starting to give testimony himself, and opinion evidence as well!"

"Objection sustained!" ruled Worsthorne in ringing tones. He loved to sustain objections for the prosecution.

Baldwin returned his attention to Sidney, with a smile. "Now, you say you think you saw the accused in your store on the afternoon of Friday the 14th of January?"

"Yes, I did."

"Well then, Sid," and Baldwin leaned closer to Sid with a friendly smile, "I'm sure that you can tell me and tell the court which of these hats my client was wearing on that occasion."

Sid looked at the hats whose display had fascinated him by their presence ever since he had entered the courtroom. There must have been some discussion regarding these hats while he had been excluded or they wouldn't be there would they? So which one was it — which one had Dan Mackenzie been wearing. Sid thought, dammit, I think it was a kind of chauffeur's hat he was wearing, but how the hell could he remember which hat after the couple of months that had passed since the incident. Well the one on the left was the closest to any memory of a hat Sid might have had. The guy had been in his store, he'd been wearing a hat, hadn't he. Christ, it was wintertime.

"You're hesitating, Sid. Don't you remember?" prompted Old Man Baldwin, no longer smiling.

"Ah . . . it was the one on the left, the flatish, wide type, with the peaked front," said Sid quickly.

"Now you are sure that's the hat Dan Mackenzie was wearing that afternoon in your store?"

Sid paused, then, "Yes — yes I am." Sid had definitely decided that was the hat.

"Thank you, Sidney," said Baldwin. "And he was in your store and he was wearing that hat — you are sure it was the accused whom you saw there?"

"Yes."

"And he was wearing that particular hat?"

"Yes." Sid was sure.

"That is all the questions I have for this witness, Your Worship," and Baldwin sat down.

"Are you calling any further witnesses or evidence, Mr. Phimester?" inquired the judge.

"No, Your Worship, that concludes the case for the prosecution," said the Crown agent.

"Mr. Baldwin, are you presenting any testimony for the defence?" was the next question.

"A mere scintilla, a very small amount thereof, sir, if I may.

"By all means — proceed. But it is getting near the noon recess, may I inquire as to how many witnesses you intend to call?"

"Very few, M'lord, only these three hats!"

"I beg your pardon? Did I hear you say three hats?"

"Yes, these three hats on the table here." And Old Man Baldwin picked up the first. "I would like to enter this hat as Exhibit A for the defence, along with the bill of sale for same, showing that I purchased this hat at the High Prairie Mercantile store two weeks ago for $9.95."

"Well, if that's what you want to do. Strange, but I see no objection." The clerk marked and entered the evidence.

Baldwin picked up the middle hat. "I swear that this hat is my own and that I have been wearing it for two years. May it be entered as Exhibit B in this case."

"Mr. Baldwin, remember that exhibits in these cases must be held in the court files until at least after any appeal period is over. You might go hatless for months," said Worsthorne, and the laughter of the courthouse crowd at this sally, pleased him mightily.

"I'll take that chance, Your Worship." Best to keep everyone in a good mood during these trials, thought Baldwin — it increases your chance of winning by five to ten percent. He picked up the third hat and paused — then, "This is the hat that Sid Kovnats has unmistakenly and unequivocally identified as the hat that was worn by the accused Dan Mackenzie when that poor man was alleged to have been in High Prairie on the afternoon immediately preceding a motor vehicle theft that took place in that town on January 14th, 1949. I would like to enter it as Exhibit C to this trial along with a bill of sale and a sworn affidavit made by Mr. Saul Martineau, the owner and proprietor of Martineau & Sons Ltd. of Peace River, which prove that it was purchased at his store at nine o'clock this morning. Except for argument that is the case for the defence."

There was a silence in the courtroom for what seemed like a minute, but which was probably only a few seconds. Time seems longer during a pregnant pause.

"I think I can dispense with hearing your argument at this time, Mr. Baldwin — I know what it is. Mr. Phimester, are you prepared to argue the validity of the prosecution's identification of Dan Mackenzie as the thief of the vehicle, in view of the fact that you do not seem to have placed him either in that truck near Wabasca, nor at the scene of the theft in High Prairie — beyond a reasonable doubt that is!"

Sandy Phimester stood up slowly, "Your Worship, I would say that I doubt that the accused may have been wearing a hat at all — there is really no evidence that he was."

"And then I would say," Old Man Baldwin was on his feet and interjecting, "that my learned friend would then be attempting to express opinion evidence himself, and he's not a witness in this trial and his case is closed."

This was tough on Worsthorne, but this time he saw what he had to do. "Objection sustained, Mr. Baldwin. Mr. Phimester, your own witness says Mackenzie was wearing a hat, and also identified a hat that could not possibly have been in High Prairie on the day in question. If he is wrong about the hat, he could be wrong about the wearer of the hat. Or are you going to tell the Court that Mr. Kovnats was talking through his hat?" More laughter from the minions.

Phimester smiled and resignedly sat down. Brown whispered to Nivens, "Screwed, booed and tattooed — in the hat!"

Judge Worsthorne rapped his gavel and said, "I find you not guilty as charged. Case dismissed. But find another way of getting back to Wabasca the next time."

Dan Mackenzie left the courtroom with his jubilant fans.

Old Man Baldwin went over to where Sid was standing with Pop Polski, stuck out his hand, smiling, and asked, "How's the wife and family, Pop?"

"They're doing okay," replied Pop, "except that Sid here, could sure use a new hat!"

# Johnny

Hal C. Sisson

I was talking to Johnny Delorme, a Woodland Cree Indian, born on a ranch near Peace River, Alberta in 1928. We were talking about his many brushes with the Canajan Moundies, primarily because he had a periodic drinking problem. Johnny was accident prone when it came to dealing with the law.

You could tell from his face that he had been in a lot of fights. He had been a boxer in the Canadian Army, and from the present placement of his nose on his physiognomy, he had lost quite a few of his ring encounters. Also he had served in the Korean war as a twenty-mile sniper (an artillery-man), and had always been involved in breaking horses, rodeos and bronc riding, none of which is conducive to one's health and looks. There were lots of broken bones and wounded knees inherent in the nature of his life style, in what he was and what he had done all his life. He was reminiscing.

"One time the cops picked me up for something. I forget

what it was. I'm trying to remember. Was it the first time they ever had them women cops? That goddamn redhead, she was after my ass all the time. She was in her glory if she could pick me up. Was it the first time I dumped them nine pigs out of the dray onto Main Street? No, that was earlier, 'cause that time I was driving a green team down Kaufman Hill. They were a bastard — nearly ran away on me; and when I got them stopped they started to buck. I think one of the reins broke. I told the cops what happened, and it was true. But they charged me anyway, likely because those pork chops was creatin' havoc all over the place. Something about negligence or driving without due care and diligence. I proved that was no musical ride and I got off. Never did find one pig." Johnny paused.

"No, I do remember now. It was the time I hit the cop car."

"You hit a cop car, Johnny?"

"Yeah, you see, I was bringin' in this old truck from Three Creeks, goin' like a bitch mink 'cause the brakes was all but shot and I knew it. Lucky I got down the hill all right, but at the bottom I see this cop car ahead of me. Well, thar weren't no reason for them to stop at this cross street, there was no red light or nothing, and nobody coming — so I didn't expect it — and anyway, like I told you, I had no brakes. The dumb buggers stopped right in front of me. What could I do? There was people on the streets. Actually, Hal, when I saw I had no alternative, I did give her a little gas as I piled into their rear end. But then the judge — it was my old friend Lloyd Levesque — did I tell you we grew up together? At least he did. Yeah, well, what could Lloyd do? Had to do something on the charge 'cause this time it was really careless driving. So he gave me a hundred-dollar fine and thirty days to pay."

"That's not half bad."

"No, but I didn't have the money, so the cops came looking for me after the thirty days 'cause I didn't pay the fine. I was sittin' in Rotary Park where I usually hung around a lot, when a cop I never saw before — musta been new in

town — came up to me where I was sittin' on the bench and asked me, 'Do you know Johnny Delorme?'
"I replied, 'Yes, I do.'
"'Do you know where he usually hangs out?' said the Moundie.
"'Well, I know some of them!'
"'Would you be willing to show me?' he says. I pretended to think it over for a moment, and then said, 'Yeah, I could do that for you.'
"'Thanks,' he says, and motions me to come along. We get into the police cruiser and start looking, and the first place I take him is over to Russ Green's place in West Peace River. We get out and come up the boardwalk. Russ is in the garden. The Moundie goes into his routine about does he know Johnny Delorme. Russ, of course, says yes he does.
"'Do you know where he is now?' the cop asks.
"'Not anymore'n you do,' Russ replies.
"'Have you seen him lately?' continues the cop. 'We're looking for him.'
"'What do you mean by lately?' Russ asks.
"'Well, like in the last few days, a week ago, whatever.'
"'Then no, I ain't seen him lately,' says Green, looking straight at me. 'The last time I seen him was maybe a couple of months ago. Why, what'd he do?'
"'Skipped out on a fine.'
"'Usually does more than that,' answers Russ. 'But next time I do see him, I'll tell Johnny you're lookin' for him. Likely he knows it anyways.'
"Cop thanks Russ and we leave. Next we go down to see Pete Blue in Philippeville and the same thing happens. Pete tells the cop, 'That sonofabitch owes me five bucks and I haven't seen him for six weeks. If you catch him, tell him he'd better pay me back or I'll bust his ass.' I pipe up and tell Pete, 'Well, if I see the sonofabitch, I'll tell him some bastard called Blue is really cheesed off 'cause he hasn't paid him, but Johnny usually has a good excuse.' Pete kinda smiles and says, 'You do that!'

"This happens a couple more places and the cop drives me around to see all my friends, until he gets tired and guesses we aren't going to find me. So he drops me at my sister's where I was staying, and thanks me for my assistance and cooperation. I told him anytime, I don't want any trouble with the police.

"Well, of course, they keep lookin' and I still ain't got the hundred bucks. Couple of days later a cop car comes to my sister's house. This time there is my new friend on the force, but there is also another cop with him. One who'd been stationed in town for a good spell. I shoulda been treatin' my sister with a little more respect, I guess, 'cause when they ask her, 'Do you know Johnny Delorme?' she says, 'Of course I do, he's my brother.'

"'Where is he?' ask the cops, and she tells 'em, 'He's upstairs drinking booze!' They came up and got me, of course, and I lost my new friend in the RCMP, 'cause he was some pissed off when he saw it was me.

"They took me down to the Magistrates Court. It was Lloyd again. He says, 'Have you got the dough that I fined you?'

"I said, 'No.'

"'You out of a job?'

"'Yes.'

"'Well, why the hell didn't you tell me you needed money?'

"I said, 'Why the hell didn't you ask me?'

"That man did a lot for me, but I don't think the cops liked him a whole bunch. On this occasion he tells the cops that his notes seemed to indicate that there had been two months to pay; and because of that clerical mix-up, that was his ruling and he would see to it that I paid up. Lloyd took me up to his house and put me to work gardening. After a couple of days the chores ran out and Lloyd said, 'That's enough. I'll fix up the goddamn fine. Now get the hell out of here and just stay out of my courtroom!'"

I was talking to Johnny Delorme again last week.

"You were in the same hospital with Lloyd Levesque when he died? I never knew that. How come, Johnny?"

"I was in for a busted leg. I was down in Faust, tighter than the pin-feathers on a prairie chicken's ass. Met up with this nutcase. He was so plastered he opened his shirt collar to piss, but not so drunk he wasn't able to blind-side me with a steel jack-all. No reason. Busted my leg real bad, so they sent me to the Peace River Hospital. Lloyd was in there with a kidney condition."

"Yeah, I remember, it killed him in the end."

"We visited back and forth. Mostly I went to see him on crutches. Then one morning they just told me he died in the night. Hell, I was talking with him the night before."

"What did you talk about?"

"Long time ago. Can't remember, really."

"Nothing?"

"Only one thing. It was funny, so I remembered."

"What?"

"He was recalling when he was back in college. Story wasn't about him, really. About his roommate. Lloyd was French Canadian but his pal was English. Took out this French girl that Lloyd introduced him to. When he came back from the date, Lloyd asked him how he made out. And basically, I remembered what Lloyd told me he said about that."

"So what did he say?"

"He said, 'Well, we got back to her apartment, and I began to neck with her. Things started to get hot, but suddenly she went as cold as a well rope, pulled away from me and said, 'Take your hands from amongst my ass, I'm not da girl for dat!'

I laughed when Johnny said that, but I'm not sure why. Probably the incongruity of the terminology. Strange thing for a guy to think of the night before he dies.

Johnny was with a small gang of cronies from Cadotte Lake when I ran into them in the alley behind Main Street. Their greeting was so friendly it was almost as if they had been looking for me.

"Sisson," they said, nearly in unison, "we glad to see you, we want to buy you a drink."

I protested both my innocence and the time of day as excuses — it was too early to be on the sauce.

"Hal, its 4:30, man. Come on, the boys were tellin' me how much they like you," said Johnny Delorme.

"Do they now?"

"Yeah, soor."

"You stick up for us wit the cops."

"Come into the Mac. We buying."

"You're not going anywhere important." I wondered how they knew.

I was surrounded, Johnny was nodding and his hand on my arm was a guiding one. To refuse was impolite and what the hell, a beer would be nice. I deserved it.

We all entered the Mac by the back door. San Francisco has the Top of the Mark, Peace River has the Back of the Mac, full name the McNamara Beer Parlour. They should never tear the place down. It should be preserved by the Heritage Sites Board or the Alberta Liquor Control Board as a museum. The place is so bad it is good. It preserves the essence of western Canadian beer emporiums as they had existed since the early part of the century. Strange — I'd slung and drunk beer in quite a few of them, and although everyone called them "parlours," I can't recall one that actually used that word in their official title or sign. Maybe I'm wrong on that but I don't think so.

Like, after drinking in a beer parlour, you could never remember the colour of the walls or the ceiling or the location of the bar or the cans. You didn't have to — they were all about the same, including the tables and chairs. These were places built for drinking beer and nothing else. You couldn't stand up to drink, you had to sit, no food was sold or allowed as it interfered with the business at hand, which was quaffing beer and lots of it. There was no music and no women. Those things had gradually changed over the years, but not the decor of the Mac. And that was good, because, like a church, you knew where you were and you knew why you were there. You seen one, you basically seen 'em all.

There were about six of us in all. One of Johnny's four buddies ordered a round, which as any beerslinger knows, consists of two glasses of beer each. Someone paid and we slowly started to shoot the shit, as was the ancient custom in all beer parlours. You could never go to a beer parlour without shooting the shit — besides drinking beer, there was nothing else to do.

Now the first beer always tastes the best, that's a known fact. Therefore it gets consumed quickly, so you can get to the second one to see if it tastes just as good — which we did. It never does. We sipped and a few raunchy attempts at humour were bandied about along with the news of the world as it affected Cadotte Lake Reserve, the goddamn Moundies and the state of noassatall and no work in the bush. Nobody wanted to trap anymore, there was no money in it. Which brought the conversation around to the hunting season.

"Lotsa Americans out in the buss right now," said Louie.

"Not safe to go in the buss right now, thats for soor."

"Yeah, you could get sot," said another of the group. The 'sh' sound in English seems to bother the Cree.

Johnny chimed in. "Saw the damnedest thing last week, on the road to Haig Lake. Bear had one of them hunters up a tree."

That got everyone's attention.

"I was driving along with Tommie Ghostkeeper, out about where the farmland is getting few and far between, when we heard a shot. A mile down the road, maybe you know that big meadow with the little creek, and that lone poplar tree in the field. You guys drive by it all the time."

"That's past Three Creeks Store, ain't it?"

"Yeah, we know it."

"Well, when we got there, standing on a big limb of that tree, about halfways up, was this hunter, and not too far below was a big brown bear, trying to climb higher. You could see that the guy had pissed his pants. He was in a bad way for shure. We stopped and I spotted his rifle leanin' against a big rock over to the left.

"'What are we gonna do?' says the old Ghost Keep, and I say, 'Blow the horn.' Tommy pressed hard on the button and, when the bear heard the horn blast, he swung his head around sharp. Bashed his face on the tree trunk, as a matter of fact. Looked at us for a few seconds and then scrambled down the tree and ran across the field into a bunch of willows along the creek."

"What did the hunter do?" someone asked.

"We were waving and yelling to him to get over to the car. You ever see those firemen slide down that pole they got in firehalls? Like in the movies, maybe. Well, he came down that tree just like that, and just about as fast. And he started to run, but instead of headin' right for the car, he heads for his gun."

"This guy had to be from the city," Louie remarked.

"But just then, the bear came out onto the bank of the creek. The hunter saw him and let out a yell. We were yelling, too, for him to run to the truck. But he stops dead in his tracks and looks all around. He was scared shitless, I guess, 'cause I think he could have made the truck, but the dumb bugger runs back to the tree. Climbs it again. Now the bear starts across the field, too, but we can only see him from the ass end. We notice something funny about his gait — wasn't natural-like. Something is the matter, his back legs are going okay, but he's sort of humping along on his front ones. Oh oh, we say, maybe he's wounded, there's something wrong up front. Maybe that hunter shot him once before we got there. Don't mess with the local denizens in their own habitat unless you know how to shoot to kill. It's a natural fact they may want to even the score — make it bears one, humans nothing."

"What was the matter with the bear?" I had to ask.

"When the bear got to the base of the tree, we could see why he had been walkin' so funny," said Johnny.

"Why?" several others asked.

"He was carrying a beaver he had got from the creek — and he set it down at the base of that poplar!" There was dead silence for maybe twenty seconds.

"You are rotten to the core, Johnny," Louie said flatly.

"Sonofabits, I'm never listening to you again," said someone else. But everyone laughed.

A hairy bear story, for Chrissakes, and we fell for it, I thought. Nice lead-in, though.

Every glass except mine was suddenly, I noticed, empty; and the table conversation had slacked off to silence. I knew they were all looking at me as I sipped my second beer.

"It's gettin' mighty dry in here," Johnny commented.

"Your problem, Johnny, is that every time you open your mouth, you think your arm has to bend at the elbow. Would it be against your religion to buy a round?"

"You know me, Hal, I always seem to be broke." He leaned over confidentially and said, "It really was nice of the boys to buy you a drink — specially when they only had enough money for one round. It likely embarrasses the hell out of them that they can't buy you another."

"I bet it does!" I replied, "but I can't help that, can I? They wanted to buy."

"True story," said Johnny, "because they like you. They always tell me you are fair in court."

"I see. So what do you think I should do?"

"Whatever you think is fair, Hal."

So I did. Three rounds later I left — right after ordering the last one and paying for them all. Left on a full table — got out fast before they could empty it. Johnny was smiling and waving as I left. He likely still had seed money in his pocket, I'm shure, to buy another round for someone. Flattery will get you somewhere!

# Double Bite

Hal C. Sisson

Johnny Delorme figured he was the toughest man who ever crapped over the heel of a boot. That is what he figured. I didn't agree with him. Some people thought Johnny was loose as ashes and twice as shifty. I didn't agree with them either. Always complex of nature, Johnny had come to the stage in his life where a good part of his normal income was derived from putting the bite on people. What were friends for if you couldn't put the touch on them. That was his attitude and periodically I was on his list.

Johnny never just walked up to the front door of my house — he was afraid of my wife. He'd phone first and try to get me on the blower. Or he'd wait till he caught me out in the yard, mowing the lawn or some such job — which was what happened on this particular day. He came limping down the grassy dike along the Peace River, and I shut off the lawn mower and fell back against the slope, welcoming a respite, although I knew it was likely going to cost me money in the long run. Johnny didn't always hit you up, sometimes he just wanted to talk, and sometimes when he was flush from odd-jobs, he played the philanthropist and gave you back a few of the bucks he had borrowed in the past. Which would it be this time?

I greeted him by asking, "How's your leg?" He had been in the Canadian Army and later enlisted in the Korean War. His main wound from those episodes was his nose, flattened against his dark brown features from too many regimental boxing matches, many of which he had won. No canvass-back Johnny. The limp came much later in his career, his leg having been broken in several places by an iron tire jack. During the ensuing operation several steel pins had been inserted and Johnny had limped ever since. This didn't stop him from riding the odd rodeo bronco. Well, eventually it did, but not for a long time anyway.

"Don't get any better. I should have got you to sue that sonofabitch!"

"Wouldn't have been any use, he didn't have a dime. Nowadays they've got legislation for the benefit of crime victims, John — but not when that happened."

"Oh yeah, I forgot. You know, that's the trouble with some Indians. We only got enough money to get drunk. Which brings me to why I came to see ya."

"I can guess why."

"Well, things haven't been goin' so hot for me lately."

"Sorry to hear that, John." I wasn't about to bite so quickly; he'd have to work a lot harder than that. There were a few moments of silence, finally broken by Johnny.

"Yeah, reminds me of the time I was right here on the riverbank, before the dike got built. I was down by Rotary Park — standin' right by the river drinking a bottle of plonk with Sonny Whitehead."

"When was this?" I asked.

"Not sure zactly. Musta been around the early sixties. Back then the cops were always chasin' me."

"Have times changed?"

"A little — maybe a lot — they don't bother old guys so

much." Johnny looked up and down the riverbank as if half expecting someone to appear, and then he continued, "I didn't see Corporal Morgan and the other Moundie coming down the bank. Sonny Whitehead did — too damn dumb to warn me, the stupid bastard. I had the bottle in one hand and the cork in the other. Morgan says, 'Aha, I caught you this time Johnny, for sure!'

"'No you ain't!' I says and shoved the cork into the bottle and flung it into the river as far upstream as I could.

"'You smart-ass Indian,' Morgan yelled, 'I may not have the evidence but we saw you drinking that wine, and I got you.'

"'What wine? And you ain't got me either, Morgan,' I said, and ran right out into the river. Well, lucky for me that I threw that bottle upstream, because as it happened it floated down right past me and I sure as hell grabbed on to it. The water was maybe only waist or chest deep, so I just stood out in the river and proceeded to knock off the rest of the bottle."

I laughed as I visualized Johnny getting drunk in the flowing river, while the cops stood on the shore watching him destroy the evidence. "What did they do?" I asked.

"Well the other horseman went back to the cruiser and I guess he radioed for help, because pretty soon here comes another cop car. Morgan is haranguing me from the bank, apparently seriously requesting me to come ashore. I just keep grinnin' at him and drinkin' the wine — I'm feeling fine." And Johnny was grinning again now as he told his tale.

"As I recall the corporal wasn't one to give up easily. What happened?"

"He got so mad he took off his breeches and came into the water after me. I hadn't figured he would do that, but he was so damn frustrated, and maybe the other cops were eggin' him on."

"And?"

"And when he waded into the river I waded out and started running down the bank as hard as I could go, the other cops right on my ass. Caught me, of course, but the bottle was at the bottom of the Peace River and the wine was at the bottom of my belly."

"Was that the end of it?"

"Hell, no. It was a Monday afternoon and magistrate's court was in session. Your old buddy Lloyd Levesque was sitting. Damn it, Lloyd was some judge all right. Too bad he's dead."

"He certainly practiced law his own way. A good partner, but actually he was the lone wolf type — his office methods would drive you up the wall."

"So the cops marched me in there to lay charges, all soakin' wet like I was. Lloyd takes a quick look at this situation and says 'What's going on here? Just slow up a bit, Corporal. Let's let the accused get a word in here. Now what happened, Johnny?'

"And I said, 'The cops made me go in the river!'"

"You are a genuine shit-disturber, John!" I interjected. "I've told you before, you can bug those guys too much you know."

"Maybe, but Lloyd got mad at that and said, 'I thought we all had a talk about leaving this man alone. He's no menace to society and I'm tired of seeing him in my court. He is soaking wet — I suggest you get him down to the hospital and have him checked out. He could get pneumonia.' Jeez were the cops mad at me, especially Corporal Morgan.

"Anyway they took me down there and Doc Takacz checked me over. I was out in ten minutes. Takacz said, 'There's nothing wrong with this man.' The hospital gave me dry clothes, and when we got outside, Morgan, boy does he chew me out. He says, 'You goddamn crap-can artist, I'm gonna get you, and I'm gonna get you good!'

"The cops take me back to the courtroom. We go in front of Lloyd again. I looked at him and I figured he was having a hard time to keep from laughing. The cops tell him I'm okay but Lloyd says, 'All right, let's hear Mr. Delorme's side of the story before we lay any charges.' You see Lloyd knew me a long time. We both came from around here and whereas I joined the army, he had joined the air force. So Lloyd asks me what happened at the hospital.

"I said, 'They threatened me!'"

This statement brought a remonstration from myself: "You're putting me on!"

"No, I'm not — as sure as I'm sittin' here — Lloyd gets even madder this time, or leastwise that's what it looked like — and he said, 'I thought I told you to leave this man alone. I'm sick and tired of this bullshit. Nothing is happening here and nothing is going to — I won't accept the charges. Case dismissed.'

"Son of a gun — they had to let me go, but I knew I was going to have to stay out of Morgan's way. Later, maybe a couple of hours, I went over to Lloyd's private office. It was after five and he was all alone.

"'Goddamn it, John!' he said. 'You nearly got everybody into shit this afternoon. You gave me a bad time with those cops. I can't keep doin' that for you. Why don't you stay out of trouble?'

"'Lloyd,' I said, 'I been tryin', but you know how it is. I been down on my luck lately. True story — I'm broke right now as I talk to you. I was wondering, Lloyd, if you could lend me twenty bucks?'

"'You are incorrigible, Johnny,' Lloyd said.

"I'm not sure what that means — but anyway, Lloyd just fumes around in his chair and stares at me a few seconds — then he whips out his wallet and takes out some money. Then he says, 'Here's forty dollars, Johnny, now get the hell out of here — I don't want to see you for a couple of months!'"

Needless to say, I had been laughing throughout Johnny's rendition of this horrendous tale, but I stopped suddenly when Johnny said, "I was wonderin', Hal, if you could lend me twenty bucks?"

# The Family Doc
## Hal C. Sisson

Doc was mad. I mean when he came into my law office, he was way past irate and into furious.

"What's the matter? Why the official visit?" I asked.

"The sonofabitch insulted my nurse," Doc replied.

"Come on in and tell me who that might be," I said, ushering him into what was laughingly referred to as the library. "Would you care to tell me about it?"

He would and he did. A dweller of Falher, a realtor, a notary public, a flyer of his own airplane, was the dastard, according to Doc. Every so often pilots must have a physical checkup to prove they are in fit condition to fly. That was the reason for Gerard's visit to Doc's Peace River office. And Doc had done just that, being a persona grata medic with whatever government agency authorized and paid for these medical checkups. This would prove Doc to have strong Liberal connections at the time, if anyone is interested, which they are not.

Doc was also the designated hitter for all the insurance

agents in the area. If you needed a physical to qualify for an insurance policy, you went to Doc. I did that several times and although it was fifteen years after WWII, Doc would say, "You were discharged from the air force as physically fit, weren't you?" "Yeah, that's right," I would reply, and that was basically it. Doc guessed my height and weight and what my grandmother died of, did the paperwork and I passed. I don't think he liked insurance companies, but then, who does?

Gerard had his checkup and went home and wrote a letter back to Doc. Gerard was a small, wiry, truculent French Canadian egomaniac. I read his letter, in which Gerard claimed that the nurse-receptionist forced him to wait for too long a period of time in the waiting room — like half an hour. He was not used to being kept waiting when he had an appointment, and he requested that Doc severely castigate the nurse for subjecting him, the Great Gerard, to such disrespectful treatment. The nurse, also his secretary, had opened and read the letter.

This effrontery was what made Doc mad — plus the added factor that he was sleeping with his nurse at the time and therefore needed to rush to her defence. I forget whether that was before or after they got married. Must have been before or he wouldn't have gotten so angry.

Doc had come to town very early in its history and therefore figured he owned all the patients for fifty miles around, an attitude which didn't sit well with other doctors. So Doc was really no one to take umbrage when it came to ego. His ego was not about to take a back seat to anyone, so in reply he had composed several pages of vituperative bad-mouthing directed at Gerard, wherein he was afraid he might be approaching libel. Would I read it with that in mind, because he wanted to publish it in the local it in the local newspaper.

I read it — read phrases like "common as owl shit" and that Gerard was so ugly flies wouldn't light on him.

"Doc," I said to him, "it's not libel unless you publish it

and you are not going to do that. But in any case, this invective is too much. It doesn't accomplish anything — I mean, telling him he is like a small fart in a wet mitten? This won't do!"

"Well, what will?" the Doc wanted to know. "You're good at this stuff, Hal — you tell me what to do."

"I'll think it over. Brevity is the soul of wit — you've heard that phrase?"

"Yes."

"So — just send Gerard a telegram."

"And tell him what?"

"Please make another appointment — I forgot to examine your head!"

But that wasn't what I started out to tell you. I wanted to tell you about Doc and the babysitter. There can be problems with new babysitters, you know. Why? Because they are accident-prone, that's why!

My wife and I were new parents — first child, about one and a half when this happened and the kid slept right through the whole thing. Thank God for that. If he had been yowling, it would have made the whole thing worse than it already was.

Okay, there's this party, and four of us, another couple and ourselves, go in my car. We hire a new babysitter for the evening, a girl, maybe fourteen years old. My wife gives her all the usual instructions. We're having a good time at the shindig, and a few drinks into the evening, about 11:30 PM, I phone home — check on things, like new parents do. No answer. Strange. Worrisome. I think about it. A few minutes later, I phone again. Still no answer. Now I'm really worried and I tell the wife. All four of us leave the party, as our friends didn't bring their car. It's too early to leave, but we gotta go. Pisses me off no end.

Anyway, I drive to our home first to check on the problem, and we all go in. Now we see why the babysitter didn't answer the phone. At first we can't find anybody but our son, sleeping calmly in the nursery. But then we hear someone sobbing, and we find the babysitter in the bathroom — stuck to the toilet seat!

Yeah, I'm not kidding. I painted the seat the week before and the paint was old style, tacky, taking forever to dry, from the outside in. We knew about it so we didn't linger on the seat; and the kid, crapper Dan, well, he was too young to go to the biffy on his own.

But the babysitter didn't know, and she went to the can, sat down to do her business, and started to read the magazines that everyone usually keeps some of in the toilet. Shades of the old outhouse. When she went to get up, her bum was stuck fast to the seat and she was scared sh..., well, she was really frightened. And now she's so embarrassed she can hardly communicate. The wives get us out of the bathroom and they try to get the girl unstuck. She won't pull loose. They try turpentine, but her screams soon make them desist in that method.

We have a conference. I go to get my tool kit while my wife phones Doc and explains the problem. I'm wondering what he's going to do, but then somebody has to do something.

I try the plumbing approach. By now, all modesty is by the boards, and I'm lying on my back at the base of the toilet, trying my damnedest to remove the seat where it is hinged to the toilet.

I hear a cab pull up and I go out front. The Doc steps out. His pants are over his pajamas and he's still in bathrobe and slippers. This is out in the boonies, so Doc has to wade through deep snow and a shallow ditch.

He is not happy.

You wouldn't know the Doc, of course, but he was at the party, too, and wasn't home long when he got the call for help. He should have stood in bed, as they say, known better than to answer the phone. At that time of night it's always an emergency or a drunken friend with phone-itis. Anyway, the Doc is there and he inspects the situation. I can see this isn't a problem he covered in medical school, 'cause he looks nonplussed, but he takes a crack at it. Talks to the girl in his best bedside manner as she sits blubbing on the seat. I'm back down on the tiles trying to release the toilet seat. Doc looks down at me past the girl's legs, with me gazing up at him. He says, "We've got to stop meeting this way..." He was a joker!

Doc places one foot on the toilet seat between her legs and braces himself with the other against the base of the bathtub. He's a specialist, I can see that. He grabs her by the shoulders and pulls. She doesn't move, but he does — his hands slip off her body and he crashes back against the far wall and falls sideways into the tub, landing hard on his right side.

I drop my wrench, jump up from under the toilet, look down at Doc lying in the bathtub and say, "I agree, you're right, let's stop meeting this way. But are you all right?"

The Doc says, "No! I think I broke my arm!"

"Bullshit," I replied.

"Don't tell me bullshit! I'm the doctor and I should know if my arm is broken. Now phone an ambulance for both of us or some way to get us to the hospital — but get me to hell out of this tub."

My friend and I ease him up by his good arm. I'll hand it to Doc. He's in a lot of pain, but he says, and this is exactly what he says, "Now you know why we're against house calls. Take my right hand and hook the thumb into my belt."

He needs some support for the arm, so we do that. We help get him out of the tub and my wife phones the hospital and asks them to send around whatever transport they are using for an ambulance. I think the hearse from the funeral parlour was doubling as the ambulance at the time.

The toilet seat finally yields to my wrench and screwdriver. Now we can get someplace, but the girl can't walk in this condition. Don't laugh! It isn't funny! That poor girl. Victim of circumstance. The hearse arrives and we help the driver carry her out in a sitting position, and the Doc crawls into the back with her.

I phone her mother and I'm saying to myself, "So okay, how am I going to varnish this over." Sorry, could I rephrase that... I start to talk to the mother, "Everything is okay, everything's all right, everything's going to be fine, but..." I told her. Even ten feet from the phone you could have heard that mother's answer. When it's 2:00 AM and your fourteen-year-old daughter isn't home and a man phones and says "Everything's all right but...," a mother is going to have a conniption fit.

"Whattaya mean 'Everything's okay?'" she shouts.

"Well," I say, giving it to her straight. Only way I suppose. "Your daughter is on the way to the hospital with a toilet seat stuck to her ass..."

The phone wouldn't have been back on the hook for five seconds before that mother was in her car and on the way to the hospital.

Oh, you want to know what happened to the sitter, how they got the seat off of her butt. Well I wasn't there and I never did find out how the medical profession perform that operation. Modern medicine has its methods I guess. These doctors are highly trained professionals and keep up on the latest surgical techniques. They can remove anything that is bugging you.

You know, the whole episode reminds me of a similar incident. Supposed to have happened in Calgary. Didn't witness it myself, of course, but I heard about it. Same situation. A wife goes to take a shower and strips bare-naked. The husband yells from the bedroom, "Don't sit on the toilet seat, I just varnished it."

Too late! She just did so. Fresh tacky varnish — she is stuck! Pandemonium. Recriminations — why didn't you tell me in time. She and he can't extricate her from her sitting position. Emergency! Well they always say call the Fire Department in case of emergency — says so on the phone book.

The fire engine speeds up to the house and several firemen in hats, raincoats and axes jump out and run into the house.

The wife yells at the husband, "They can't see me naked like this — quick, give me something to cover myself."

The husband throws her his large Stampede ten gallon hat and she puts it on her lap.

A fireman comes rushing into the bathroom, axe in hand. Looks around, assesses the situation, then says to the husband "I think we can save your wife, but the cowboy is a goner..."

Doc's arm eventually healed of course, and he carried on to perform many other operations — but perhaps none as noteworthy as that of the toiletseatectomy. I told you Doc was a joker and I remember another thing he did. Involved a big baboon, a drill baboon was what he said it was if memory serves me. He was a big one all right, and why or how Doc owned him I never knew. Kept the animal in a strong mesh cage adjoined to his garage. He let the animal out on occasion, but he didn't have enough time to devote to the baboon, and the poor beast in his semi-isolation was unpredictable. I was scared to get anywhere near him. He had bitten more than one person — but no one laid charges out of friendship for their doctor.

Well, one time Doc locked the baboon in his garage where he had more space to roam than in his cage. In the garage was Doc's new Buick. Unfortunately, Doc had also overlooked a case of beer in one corner.

The baboon soon located it, smashed off some of the tops and proceeded to get pissed. Then, in a drunken frenzy, it got hold of a ball-peen hammer and pounded the living shit out of the Buick. Roof, hood, windshield — the lot. In the morning the Doc went out to the garage to tend to the baboon, and found the Buick looking like it had been hailed on from twenty miles up by hailstones as big as baseballs. The baboon was lying on the cement floor, groaning. The Doc walked over and booted the ape in the ass. The baboon got up, and holding his aching head with one hand and his butt with the other, walked over to a bottle of beer standing upright by the front of the car. He knocked off the top and gulped it down.

"What could I do?" Doc asked me. "I've had worse hangovers than that sonofabitch and wasn't smart enough to save a snort for the morning." Doc hugged the baboon and found some more booze and they wound up totally smashed for the rest of the day.

About two weeks later Doc lucked out. A big summer storm was brewing and he had left the car out in the driveway. It hailed for half an hour, and a few days later some insurance company got taken for a ride — figuratively speaking — in the Buick — for hail damage. Doc got a new Buick out of the deal and the baboon got donated to a zoo, and they were both better off.

In earlier times I think you had a far greater opportunity to become more familiar with your family doctor.

# Gazebos and Dreams
## Dwayne W. Rowe

The Lincoln Continental, sunroof open, glided across the field to the idling tractor and my wife Roseanne, looking like the fashion consultant she was, stepped out carrying a silver tray. She spread a linen cloth on the vast trunk, and we ate our lunch of shrimp, green salad, and sipped the dry, white wine.

We were on our farm at North Star in Alberta's Peace Country. For the past five years, our neighbours had become accustomed to her elegant style of catering and it continued to amuse them. On the adjoining farm, Conrad Nordstrom disced over a fresh, black strip near the fence just so he could grin and wave. Roseanne, the former model, who first saw a cow milked at the Edmonton Storyland Valley Zoo, waved back.

My Swedish grandfather, returning to Canada, his adopted country, after a brief hiatus known as The Great War, homesteaded in the Battle River Country in 1919 then bought more land over the years. Two of my uncles, Oscar and George, had spent their entire lives on those 960 acres until the combined forces of arthritis, cataracts and sixty years of exposure to grain dust conspired to demand payment and agreed to an extension, on one condition — their immediate retirement from farming. It was unthinkable that outsiders move onto the land, so in 1978 my cousins and I, together with another uncle, cleaned out our bank accounts, took out mortgages, signed stacks of personal guarantees and bought the family farm, together with its reliable but mainly antique machinery. Our band of co-venturers had all been reared on or near the farm, but years and distance had intervened. In the interim, I had become a lawyer, then criminal court judge, and the others — Brian, a dentist, Terry, an airline executive, Morris, a personnel director, Alvin, a petroleum drilling specialist. And Uncle Knute, man for all seasons, born and raised on that very farm, but who now lived in the Big City and worked in the publishing business.

Each spring and fall, the arrival of which varied wildly according to a never understood timetable, we went in twos and threes or all at once to sow and to reap. Skills long dormant returned slowly, sulking like mules, and had to be coaxed and beaten. We went to seminars, devoured farm literature, studied about herbicides, pesticides and sometimes contemplated suicide. Friends, former schoolmates, neighbours, old and new, came by to sample our own special brand of coffee, affectionately named "Old Guteater." They gave advice, loaned us tools and equipment and stepped in during the crunch when things went wrong. Machinery balked, then broke. Cursing our useless university degrees, we huddled around a fallen implement, kicking tires and damning whatever souls these useless, shirking hunks of steel possessed. After the season, whether planting or harvesting, we returned to our homes, three hundred or even five hundred miles away to wait for time to pass until nature again demanded our presence. Uncle Knute, sentry-like, often would remain on the farm and telephoned us with reports of impending riches or doom.

Professional practices suffered. Partners grumbled. Clients, patients and employers blustered and threatened. Incomes plummeted. Holidays were spent on the farm and whatever miserable profits accrued went to the mortgage companies and to the credit unions, ruled by farmers with the cold, grey eyes of bankers.

One night after harvest, we went to town, cousins and wives, uncles and aunts. Returning to the farm at 3:00 AM, we convinced Roseanne to holler into an empty rain-barrel. She leaned inside, legs kicking over the rusty rim, and hollered until Uncle Oscar awoke, mistaking those banshee-like echoes for the leading edge of a vicious hailstorm. Brushing away disbelief upon learning the origin of the cacophony, he dubbed her Rosie Rainbarrel and the name stuck.

Rosie visited around the area, herding that oversized Lincoln down market roads and across pastures. She discovered berry farms, learned about crop rotation, zero tillage and the importance of weather. She gathered recipes from local women and stood in line at odd hours in various implement dealerships searching out arcane parts for our deteriorating machinery. Ah, our machinery! Like salmon at the end of a spawning run — noble but decaying. Rosie watched prices rise and fall, ordered fuel, picked up supplies in town, cooked exquisite meals and delivered exotic lunches in the Lincoln. She planted tulips around the house. Tulips! Tulips in a community where survival had been the name of the game for sixty years and esthetics were just silly. However, she trimmed hedges, nurtured roses, painted equipment sheds in gentle pastels and built a wishing well from a plan she found in a magazine.

Still, she longed for a gazebo. An elegant gazebo from which sequestered space one could watch the mosquitos snarl and buzz but never penetrate. A gazebo, rising from the plain like a small temple, from where one could look out at the northern summer days hanging on almost forever. Next year, I told her. And my partners smiled.

Roseanne came to worry about breakdowns, our dwindling capital, the poor crops and the even poorer weather. She squealed at the sight, sound and smell of top-grade wheat pouring, full-bore, from the spout of the rickety combine. Dust, whether from grain or dirt, riled her asthma so she wore a designer mask and took antihistamines.

Despite interest rates that hit twenty percent, drought and frost, we survived — putting in everything, taking out nothing, except comradeship, the savour of fatigue at day's end and the laughter. Always the laughter and the outrageous practical jokes, some of which were reactivated from childhood and perfected by the fine tuning of immaturity that comes with growing older. Often we talked until dawn, tongues made furry by too many cigarettes and quarts of "Old Guteater."

By 1983, it took about two bushels of wheat to rent a video or buy a pack of smokes. The entire farming industry was in crisis and the overall situation demanded a return, on our part, to reality. At a sad winter meeting our group gathered. The cards were laid out on the table. Brains were trump that day and the hearts fell, trick by trick. We agreed to sell out to our neighbours.

At my law office, a file, acquired covertly over the years, was tucked away in a filing cabinet. It contained a myriad of plans, prices, styles, designs and colours, for lots and lots of graceful, classical gazebos. One day in April of 1983, when we last sat on the porch at the farm, I showed Roseanne the file. She looked out at the yard, the wishing well, the places where tulips would later grow, and she cried. For a lot of reasons, I suspect — but mostly for the gazebo that never was.

# A Patient's Progress

Hal C. Sisson

## Hospital Discharge Report:

Mr. Hal Sisson is being discharged from the UNIVERSITY HOSPITAL today following Coronary Artery Bypass x 4 *Complications and Problems:* Had one episode of low blood sugar (1.9) on the accuchek machine. This was done because patient was vague, drowsy, confused and hallucinating. Orange juice was given and blood sugar went up to 4.1. Previous blood sugar Sept. 15/91 −5.5 per laboratory specimen. Please continue to follow B.S. levels.

## Patient's version of the same Blood Sugar episode:

The night before they perform major surgery, they take you down to the Post-OP room, where they have half-a-dozen bad ass cases hooked up to tapocketa-tapocketa-Walter Mitty machines that you wouldn't believe if you didn't see them personally. That's why they show them to you: so that when you come to in a haze of dope you won't freak out and scare yourself to death. They have a lecturer there who uses one of the recent operatees as an exhibit to illustrate the various machines to which your life support system will be attached. They have large hoses coming out of every aperture known to the human body, and from some which have been newly created for the purpose.

A Mr. Lund, who had somehow managed to obtain this coveted role as Exhibit A for the doctor's defence, had a couple of tubes down his throat and into his lungs, through which oxygen was pumped in and out. The lecturer kept saying, "You feel fine, don't you, Mr. Lund?" But you couldn't really tell because Mr. Lund couldn't talk, and he looked like a geritol cowboy from the Streets of Laredo, all dressed in white linen and cold as the clay.

There were two of us, the next day's quota, taking the guided tour, along with near and dear relatives. Mentally, I took the attitude that I was only auditioning for the next day's role and might not get the part. Why the relatives voluntarily chose to be present I'm not sure. One of a thousand definitions of love, I suppose. My fellow patient was interesting. I had heard his history only by chance — two doctors talking outside my ward room. Apparently the cardiologist in charge of his case had placed him on the treadmill for that test, and in the midst of same, he had instructed the nurse to halt the procedure. "Get him off the machine," the cardiologist ordered. The man asked why? The cardiologist stated brusquely, "Because I can tell that you are already in danger of a heart attack and there is no use pressing our luck just to find out how really bad the condition may be. You are going to have to have surgery!"

The man said, "But doctor, I am a Jehovah's Witness and we don't believe in surgery!"

The cardiologist replied, "Well, you do have a choice — you can be a Jehovah's Witness until about next Monday, and then you'll be a dead one, or you can have bypass surgery and probably live another ten years. Make up your mind?" As the doctor turned to leave the room, apparently the man gave up his religion then and there. When he now saw the machinery and equipment in the Ops Room, I can't say what his thoughts may have been, but he was still opting for medical science. Of course, one could always pray, but as hockey mouthpiece Don Cherry once said about drug testing hockey players, "I don't care much about that; the guy I want tested for drugs is the surgeon who is about to perform open-heart surgery on me." Good point!

But I was about to relate to you the events of the night they woke me up once too often from a hard-gained sleep. Each day they had jerked out some apparatus previously inserted into the bodily life support system, until all that was left were the stitches in the chest and leg wounds. Actually they had used staples. The night nurse carefully removed each of the seventy or so of these, while my wife and daughter watched with fascinated interest. Didn't hurt them much; in fact, it didn't hurt me particularly either. They were replaced by what looked like short strips of thin transparent velcro, leaving a long neat scar. A sigh of relief to be done with the paraphernalia, some kind of sedative, and I drifted off to sleep.

It is the nurses' job to administer the attention necessary to care for, correct and alleviate medical situations in hospital wards after operations. Nothing is sacred and no modesty need be displayed. So, sometime later, I figure about two hours, I was awakened by someone shaking my shoulder and peering down into my face. A young female voice was speaking my name. My eyes slowly focused and stared for many seconds upon a tall blonde beauty in dim light. I could make out bright red, full lips over good white teeth, short curly blonde hair which seemed to continually fall over her right eye, forcing her to toss her head in that direction in order to see with both clear blue eyes. Maybe it was Veronica Lake, I figured. An enameled label on her nurses' uniform identified her as Student Nurse Candice Somebody;

obviously too young ever to have heard of that movie star and her famous hairdo. There was no one else around. I gathered from what Candy was telling me that she was conducting something called an orientation check of her patients for the evening. Was I in some sort of oriental hospital?

She asked me my full name but not my hospital serial number. I stared at her a lot longer than I should have. Surely to god they know my name I thought. Apparently taking this silence for non-comprehension on my part, Candy continued, "What hospital are you in, Mr. Sisson?"

Well I hadn't been going to movies for over fifty years for nothing. I replied, "The Royal Rangoon Military Hospital in Singapore, of course!"

"What did you say?" she asked, startled. I repeated the information and added, "but I don't know what the hell you are doing here. If the Japs overrun this position, I wouldn't want to be in your shoes. You aren't going to enjoy what they will likely do to you — and I'm not talking about pillage!"

"Mr. Sisson, answer me," said Candy, "what year is this?"

"It's 1940, of course! Now get me a subaltern in here. I'm ordering that all you nurses be sent to the rear for your own safety. My service revolver is over there on the chair and I don't want to have to use the last two bullets on you and me!"

"Sir, you are confused, you are in a modern Canadian hospital and they have recently operated on you. It is 1991."

"So I've been wounded? When did they operate?"

"A few days ago. Now I'm going to have to check your blood sugar. I suspect it must be away down because you are hallucinating."

"It's not me that is confused Miss, Candice, that's your name?"

"Yes."

"It is you that is confused!" But she wouldn't admit it; and went for help, returning with a male orderly.

I told him that I wanted all nurses evacuated to the rear, out of danger of a possible counterattack. Candy countermanded my orders and told him to help her take a sample of my blood, so she could check the sugar content.

I let her do it, not wanting to admit the subterfuge. They have a sort of triangular needle which they jab into the fatty part of one of your thumbs or fingers, then squeeze drops of blood onto a microscope slide; they compare this to other slides showing varying concentrations of blood sugar. The anticipation of the jab is the worst — it doesn't really hurt that much, and I didn't want to blow the gaff on what was shaping up into a good scam. After Candy had jabbed three or four times and couldn't seem to draw blood, I wasn't so sure. I began to think she might suspect me and was having a little revenge. If the Royal Rangoon Hospital is anywhere, it is somewhere in Burma, not in Singapore. But few in Canada would know where it is, so she certainly wouldn't have caught that mistake. But no, she finally struck blood, and lo and behold she said it did register low sugar, and that this must be the reason for my ramblings.

She left and got another student nurse — Shelly she said was the name.

"Hullo," I said, "You're back! I'm telling you girls we should all get the hell out of here. Candy, you are a Red Cross nurse, aren't you?"

"No, I'm not."

"No need to hide it. And I know you Red Cross nurses are the best. You will do anything for a soldier in his time of need in a situation like this."

"We do whatever we can, Mr. Sisson, and right now we are trying to correct your confused state of mind. Now I want you to drink this." And Candy opened a canister of orange juice, poured in two paper containers of white sugar, stirred same and put it to my lips.

I was on a non-sugar diet but so what!

"Then there is something you can do for me, Candy," I said. I reached for her hand and pulled her closer to me.

"What is it?" she asked.

"Well I wouldn't want this to get around the mess — but, well, you see . . . " I hesitated, then blurted it out, "I'm a virgin!"

"What — what are you suggesting?"

"Look, if we get through this together, I swear I'll never tell anyone, and if we don't and the enemy wipes us out, then who the devil will care or know the difference, Candy?"

"Mr. Sisson, if I didn't know the state of your mind, I would have to say that your remarks are very rude indeed, and entirely uncalled for. I have a boyfriend to whom I am engaged, a dentist, and he would not take kindly to your making such improper suggestions, I can tell you."

"I'm sure a dentist wouldn't, Candy, but then I can offer you a lot more than he can. Get rid of the dentist. He'll only fill the wrong cavity! I have a very big gopher ranch near Moose Jaw, Saskatchewan. We could go there after the war and live in luxury. I'm very rich."

"Money isn't everything by any means, sir — now, come-on, get out of bed. Shelly and I will take you down the hall. I want to test the amount of oxygen in your blood."

Well, I knew the machine she was talking about. You stuck your finger in a sort of clothes-pin affair and it registered the amount of oxygen on a digital scale. They have a lot of new machines now. One is shaped like a small gun. They put the barrel in your ear and pull the trigger and it takes your temperature immediately. I was deathly afraid of becoming constipated and having them decide to give me an enema. God knows where they would put the tube.

As we passed the biffy on the way out of the room, I asked to go to the latrine — which they allowed me to do. I had to think this over. After a few moments Candy knocked on the door. "What are you doing in there, Mr. Sisson?" she asked.

"I'm putting on my uniform," I replied. Then I let out a loud yell and charged out of the can as fast as I could. "My God, they really got me. Look at this chest wound, and this gash down my left leg! Son-of-a-gun, you weren't kiddin' Candy, when you said they had to operate on me. We all gotta get outta here. Those bastards mean business. This is a shaky-do if I ever saw one!"

Candy and Shelly grabbed an arm each and started me down the hall. I tested 93 on the oxygen content bit. Not bad. On the way back we passed the desk of the head night nurse. We all stopped. "What's going on here?" this older paragon of medical virtue intoned.

"Mr. Sisson is confused, Matron," Candy informed her. "His blood sugar is very low."

"And I'm telling you," I said, straight-faced, "that they don't realize the danger we are all in from counter-attack. And unless you are a nymphomaniac yourself, you'll get out of here too, along with all these girls."

Whether she gave them some kind of signal or not I don't know, but they urged me on into my private ward and into bed.

"Look, Hal —that is your first name, isn't it? —you really have to realize where you are. Look around. This is a modern hospital room, not a front-line casualty ward. See here, we have all this equipment; you even have a TV set."

"A what?"

"A television. Here, I'll turn it on for you and prove we are in 1991, not in some 1940 war zone." Candy flicked the power switch and on came the idiot box. As blind luck would have it the program in progress was "The World at War," a BBC rehash of WWII. Soldiers were storming out of attack boats and up the beaches into heavy machine-gun fire. Shells were exploding and men were dropping all around.

"What did I tell you, Candy? Can't you see what's happening? But how are they getting all these pictures of the action. Damn it all, now they'll be able to rate your performance. Won't be anywhere to hide."

"No, no, no, no, no —those were taken by camera men a long time ago, forty-five years ago. That's not happening today. Its history you are watching."

Candy switched programs and hit a commercial. A picture cartoon of the A & W Root Bear waddling down a desert road, pointing to a giant double cheeseburger on top of a butte, all for $1.49.

Candy said, "Now, that's reality. That is a present day commercial for A & W right there on the screen."

"And you are telling me that I'm confused! Candy, you're shell-shocked. Tell me one thing then. If this is 1991 — did we win the war?"

"Why yes, we did," she answered.

"You mean we won for this stuff? For a fat-assed bear and a double cheeseburger for $1.49? Come off it, I don't believe you!"

They switched off the TV. It wasn't helping them prove their point. The student nurses retired to the far end of the room, way past the end of my bed.

"Do you think this is a put-on?" I could hear one of them say.

"Well, no, I don't, the odds don't favour that. Look, my dad is about sixty-five and this guy is older than he is."

"So?"

"So old people don't do stuff like this on purpose."

"Yeah, he's genuinely confused, hallucinating from out of somewhere in his past."

"Let's just humour him and try and get him settled back to sleep for the night."

Not a bad idea, I thought to myself. That's what I was doing in the first place. Candy, you were the one who was touring the wards waking people up to ask them who they were and whether they were sleeping well. You wanted some confusion, you got it.

The beautiful young nurses came back to my bedside. "Well, Hal," Candy said, "go back to sleep. We'll all get out of the front-lines tomorrow, and if it is possible maybe we can all go back to your ranch in Saskatchewan with you."

"Yes," chimed in Shelly, "except there is one thing. If we do, I don't want to ride any horses. I don't like to ride horses."

I nodded my head at her. "That's okay, Shelly," and I remembered an old rhyme from the days I spent in burlesque, which I quoted to them:

> *I do like a girl who will go for a ride,*
> *In a train or a plane or a car,*
> *But a girl who'll ride horses, and ride them astride,*
> *Is stretching a good thing too far! . . .*

I thought I heard a double gasp as they both left the room, and I'll never know if they thought that was funny. Smiling, I eventually drifted back to sleep, perchance to dream — of getting out of that intensive-care hospital ward. The next morning I got my wish. The usual medical entourage made the rounds of their patients. My doctors had read the night-nurse report regarding my alleged confused hallucinations. They started asking me questions, like "what is your full name and what hospital are you in?"

"Just hold it, fellows," I burst out, "right there! I'm not ready for the rubber room!" Then I told them my version of the Bombay Idiot episode. I'll say this, they laughed. But better still, they said, "You are ready to leave." And they kicked my ass out of that hospital into the cold, cold street, that very day.

I went gladly, albeit a little sadly. I really would have liked to go to the Moose Jaw gopher ranch with Candy and Shelly. I hope they missed me on the next night shift. They were doing their duty and a good job, but a small part of my sadness was in thinking that such a ruse may have worked mainly because the young tend to think of age as a state ranging somewhere between senility and stupidity; when actually old age and treachery can very often overcome youth and skill!

# A Very Public Affair

Dwayne W. Rowe

Although it would be difficult for most people living south of the 55th parallel to accept, it wasn't until the mid-seventies that weddings in the Manning area were the subject of invitations. Before then, the way the system worked was that a couple, having decided to get hitched, would tell a few friends and relatives, and then proceed to slap up a few handprinted posters down at the theatre, cafe and bus depot. The wording on the poster simply announced the necessary details and then stated in bold letters: **COME ONE – COME ALL**. The "invite," as it was called, was then overtly extended to anyone who could read or, failing that, was fortunate enough to have someone to interpret for him.

Ordinarily, by today's standards, it would seem to be an impossible task to estimate the amount of food needed at the reception or the size of the banquet room for such a gathering, but it was easy back then. Everyone except old boyfriends and girlfriends of the betrothed, members of the participating families who openly hated each other, or those out fighting fires in the summer, would attend. Since the food was all homemade, it's not like there was some snotty, androgynous caterer with a weird accent to worry about — the kind that fifty extra spur-of-the-moment guests could send flouncing off in an uncontrollable hissyfit.

Since the premature and oft-lamented retirement of Joe Pecker, Fred Prick and the Fiddling Farts, the choice of an orchestra to play for the dance was limited to The Rhythm Kings, the hot new band of the fifties. The choice of the hall was dictated by the geographical location of the bride's home. If she lived closer to Hotchkiss than Manning, then the metal-clad Quonset hut on the local sportsgrounds was the venue. If she lived betwixt North Star and Deadwood then it depended on whether it looked like rain, because the North Star hall leaked.

During the long, dry summer of 1958, one young lady succumbed to the blandishments of a big-city Bank Manager, up in that country on temporary assignment, and agreed to become Mrs. Banker. The groom-to-be, an older fellow of about thirty, talked her into restricting the wedding to invited guests only and they sent out formal-looking invitations, with a little sissy envelope enclosed that had on it: RSVP. Within two days, the putative Mrs. Moneybags was the subject of — as they say in libel suits — calumny, contumely, degradation and humiliation, all tending to bring her unsullied reputation into disrepute. That kind of snobby behaviour was completely unacceptable to the community and the reaction was spontaneous, abrupt and formidable. Rae Simpson, the local telephone operator, who ran the phone system from a room just off her kitchen, was driven to exhaustion putting calls through at all hours of the day and night to the home of the unfortunate young lady. To make things worse, word leaked out that a Big-Town band from Peace River had been hired to play at the dance which again — horrors! — was restricted to an approved list of guests. The pressure mounted and emissaries were appointed by the assembled throng of males at the pool hall to talk some sense into the future groom.

The fact that an orchestra — as any four instrument-playing yokels were called — was to come from Peace River was, in itself, a major faux pas. The boys in those northern bands had an unofficial boundary arrangement that was adhered to fairly strictly, except if it was the wedding of a close relative in the other band's stomping grounds. Any other poaching was dealt with pretty swiftly. It was like Harold Ballard, after reading an April Fool's news story about Baffin Island wanting an NHL franchise getting all het up about it and then phoning *The Globe and Mail* to announce he would sue for infringement of his territorial franchise rights, what with Pangnirtung being so close to Toronto. The chosen envoys met with the prospective groom at Fong's cafe and, men to man, tried to point out the error of his ways. The banker, after having wised up to several scams by local farmers, like borrowing neighbours' cattle or moving the same wheat around to different granaries to enhance their net worth during a loan audit, was a pretty wily fellow. He played a little poker now and then down at Black Mike's garage and he decided to call their bluff and then to up the ante. He conceded that the band from Peace River was a mistake but offered instead to bring up Happy Russell and his Country and Western Orchestra from Edmonton.

Now, Happy Russell himself didn't play a lick on anything except when he tooted the horn on his big Cadillac convertible every year in the Edmonton Exhibition parade. But, Happy was a crafty impresario, honing his master showman skills about the same time as Ed Sullivan, and he had put together a dynamite show that toured up and down the province. He had singers, steel guitar pickers and a comedy act that relied heavily on jokes about piles, diarrhea, toilet paper and breaking wind. Any time Happy Russell came to town it was a sellout, like Garth Brooks today, only the tickets went for a buck and a half.

In the face of the banker's startling proposal, the meeting broke up and the men decided, quite wisely, to defer to the womenfolk, who arranged another meet. This one took place at the farm of Baba Kostash, not only an elder but a stronger and a smarter. Several hours of heated discussion followed, one part of which prompted Mr. High Interest Rates to stretch himself up to full length and declaim, "But it's none of your goddamn business." Within minutes, the man broke down in the face of the ensuing onslaught spearheaded by the bulky Baba, red-eyed, veins-a-poppin' and, when it looked like inevitably being on the receiving end of some serious violence, he capitulated graciously: "Enough, old woman, we'll invite the whole frigging town."

    The poor sap had failed to appreciate a salient point ingrained in the local culture. It's not like he was going to have to write himself a loan to pay for the nuptials — the bride's family always paid for the whole shebang, even if they had to sell off a quarter section and a dozen pigs to do it. Fortunately, the wedding went off smooth as flaxseed and the wedding dance at the Agricultural Hall was one of the best in recent memory. The Rhythm Kings fiddled, picked, plucked, drummed and squoze the old squeezebox like their careers were on the line — which, to some extent was true, as throughout the evening the spectre of Happy Russell was drifting like smoke around the room. The master of ceremonies stayed pretty well sober until the end of the dance and there were only three fist fights begun in the stag line at the back of the hall. The bride and groom left on their honeymoon to the sincere and rousing cheers of the crowd. The sun came up at 3:00 AM in that wonderful north country and by then the bleary-eyed wedding revelers had accomplished what the Americans could have done in Vietnam — simply by declaring a victory and going back home.

    For me, as a perpetually impecunious teenager, the most beautiful sight in the world was the morning sun glinting off those hundreds and hundreds of beer bottles scattered around the hall grounds, lying in the short grass, glistening with dew, waiting to be scooped up, chucked in a burlap sack and turned into real, hard cash at the earliest opportunity. The whole bottle business was made possible by the fact that liquor could not be served legally at any function without a permit. The kicker was —you couldn't get a permit unless it was going to be a private function with some kind of restrictions on attendance. And, since around Manning there never was anything other than a public wedding, there was no point in applying for a permit.

The RCMP would drop by once during the wedding dance and then go home. If it was raining, they would stay inside the car and paint the windows of the hall, back and forth, up and down, for a few seconds with that big, powerful, authoritarian spotlight. The room would go stiff and quiet, nobody breathing, dancers frozen in position, just like the Russkies on their submarines when the Canadian boys in the Argus anti-sub patrols lashed their Commie hulls with some super sonar to scare the crap out of them. The mandatory, yet brief, attendance by the police was made possible because the protocol was that if you wanted a drink you went outside the hall and drank inside a vehicle or maybe sat on the ground, leaned against a tree and had a few. That way, there was no flouting of the law in full view of others who were also flouting the law. There was no local prohibition against driving while impaired or even outright drunk, but true friends always prevented people from getting behind the wheel of their vehicles if it was apparent they were in the throes of alcohol-induced automatism.

Back then, there were no fancy devices like hand-held alcohol roadside testers or breathalyzers. The fact is that any Mountie stopping a drunk and demanding that he get out of the car and "blow" or provide any kind of sample of bodily substance was going to get punched out and probably pissed on. However, there were still some laws in force which were generally acknowledged as contributing to the fabric of civilized society. Being caught with open liquor inside a car was about the worst offence in the book. Such a transgression led to swift confiscation of all of the booze and a hefty fine of $15 plus another two bucks for court costs, handed out in open court by a disapproving magistrate. The audience would snicker and poke each other in the ribs as the nervous defendant would scuffle back and forth, enter a plea of guilty and then stare straight ahead while His Worship – referred to behind his back as His Horsewhip – delivered, for the millionth time, The Lecture.

As is often the case when the government attempts to regulate human behaviour, there were numerous examples of creative scofflaws who turned the whole thing into a contest between them and the police. There were some individuals with a God-given mechancial aptitude who went to great lengths to be able to transport booze inside a vehicle. One enterprising fellow installed an auxiliary windshield washer container with a separate pump and hooked it up to a hose that led to a shot glass fitted into a special bracket, positioned directly under a spout. The flow was regulated by a knob-type switch mounted on the dash inside the radio panel. Sometimes, he would get his booze control mixed up with the volume knob and instead of getting a boost to the monotone of Johnny Cash droning out over the airwaves courtesy of CKYL radio, out would come a hefty dollop of rum and coke. After thirty miles of Old Johnny belting out that one note of his, the rum came in handy. One time, he mixed up his containers during a refill and when he went to squirt the windshield it not only didn't wash away the bugs, but, being Lamb's Navy Rum, all sweet and sticky, instead of ammonia and detergent, it made things worse by attracting more insects. Unfortunately, he didn't notice the mix-up until he had downed a half-dozen shots of Windex from his other tank.

Other people cut holes in an armrest in the back seat and covered it with a fur seatcover with a hidden slit which could be pulled apart, opening the way for storage of a few dozen beer. But, the majority recognized the supremacy, if not the majesty, of the law against illegal possession of liquor, and simply tossed out the remnants before heading off in the car. So, there were all kinds of bottles, empty, full, half-full, just chucked out on the ground. Sometimes, the people at the dance, after a few trips outside to have a snort, would forget where they stashed a jug of wine and it would be found by Ray Lovlin and me during our Morning After Mop-up. We didn't drink ourselves in those days, being highly skilled ballplayers perpetually in training, so we sold off the wine, beer and spirits at a cut rate — which was fair, considering that we sometimes mixed together a few different brands or types of stuff in one bottle.

There were a few benchmarks in a young man's life — starting to shave, getting a driver's license, and being able to take a girl to a wedding dance. Getting the family car involved swearing an oath in blood that you would never, ever, ever, suffer, permit, acquiesce, or allow liquor inside that vehicle — even if you had to kill a lifelong friend to prevent it. The next big problem was in finding a girl to take to the dance. Without a girl, a fellow had to hang out at the back of the hall in the Stag Line, puffing away like crazy on Export A cigarettes and running outside every few minutes to watch the older fellows chug-a-lug rotgut out of their "mickeys" and talk about which girl had the pointiest titties.

Unfortunately, for the amateurs in matters of female conquest, their lot was to do little else but stand around and watch the Lotharios harvest the blossoms. Typically, a group of single men standing in a tightly packed group would start to play Cock Of The Walk and/or I'M THE MEANEST SONOFABITCH IN THE VALLEY. I don't remember one single dance in ten years at which there wasn't a major fight. I am not talking about those piddly-assed scuffles you see on the tube when Luc Robitaille and Doug Gilmour slap each other on the side of the helmet and then pretend to struggle free from the linesmen when they really are grateful as hell those guys showed up. The kind of brawls that took place at every dance were held outside the hall and the combatants went at it like John Wayne and Lee Marvin in "Donovan's Reef." Some guys fought over and over throughout the years, like the antagonists in Chekov's, *The Duelists*.

There were fighters in their sixties and seventies, grizzled old buggers, survivors of tough times in a harsh land and a world war or two. They would flail away, tiring quickly but relying on some form of muscle memory to try to do some of the kind of harm they used to be able to do without even thinking about it. The ringside watchers would keep track of the wins, losses and even the draws —which were declared when the brawlers simultaneously knocked each other flat-on-his-ass-stupid.

Sometimes the warfare was tribal in nature and whole families would whale away at each other out back of the hall while the women alternately begged them to stop or egged them on. I grew to love the smell of testosterone in the early morning. Now and then, the women would start fighting and, being more direct than men, wouldn't bother to go outside but began kicking, clawing and punching right on the dance floor. One bride, defending her father's honour in the face of an outrageous slur that he couldn't handle his booze —a man who at that precise moment was outside lying flat on the ground, face down in a puddle —hammered her bridesmaid with a right cross sending her sprawling into a big punchbowl of jellied salad. The semiradiant bridal attendant emerged enraged, dripping, her lovely gown soaked —a damaged dandy in aspic.

But sometimes, despite the fighting and the bickering, a dance broke out. The air would grow hot and heavy and smoky and dusty while the fiddles, guitars, accordion and drums banged out a great Polka, Schottische, or some new-fangled rock and roll. Then there would come the Old Time Waltz which nobody under fifty could dance to, followed by a slow dance like the Mom and Dad Waltz by Lefty Frizell. If a guy did have a girl at the dance, she could dance with other people before, but not during, the Supper Waltz which was played exactly at midnight. The Golden Rule, religiously observed by all females, was you danced the Supper Waltz and went home with the guy what brung you.

The big, folding tables from the back would be hauled

out and set up, covered by long vinyl tablecloths. The food would be brought out and piled on and on and on until the mile-long tables were groaning and quivering from the accumulated weight. There were devilled eggs, soups, pickles, berry pies, beef, hams, yams, chickens, turkeys, ducks, geese, salads, corn on the cob, cabbage rolls, perogies and rice-with-raisins pudding. After scarfing down a half a hog and a few chickens each, washed down with brutally powerful coffee, the crowd would push back their chairs, groan, belch and start hollering for the newlyweds to give a speech. After the profuse thanks to Moms and Dads, Grannies, Gramps and everyone else, the band would strike up the appropriate schmaltz from Strauss and the couple would twirl around the edges of the floor while people pressed money into their hands or stuffed bills into folds of the bride's dress or down her neckline.

Sometimes, the bride would dance with a basket over her arm into which money was thrown and she would be flushed with happiness at the sight of all that filthy lucre. It was forbidden to kiss the bride due to some unfortunate past incident when a sloppy drunk insisted on giving the bride a French kiss. He ended up losing part of his tongue in the process which, due to the pain caused by the broken nose, he didn't notice until the next morning. On occasion, the rewards were such the young couple could completely outfit their new home with waterless cookware and MelMac unbreakable dishes or pay cash for a new set of harrows.

The orchestra, collectively but arbitrarily, decided when it had played enough and they would segue from a polka into that rousing evening-closer, "Show Me The Way To Go Home." It was a great song and everyone joined in, "I'm tired and I want to go to bed. I had a little drink about an hour ago and it went right to my head."

Since it got light very early in the summer, any petting and necking had to be done in that crucial hour between the end of the dance and first light. Experienced roving hands knew enough not to be discouraged by a false dawn.

In terms of feeling really stupid, there is nothing like being parked on what you thought was an abandoned trail, the windows all fogged up in the car, when suddenly the sun comes blazing through like a fireball and a tractor pulling a disc rolls up alongside. The farmer leans over the fender of the tractor and waits until you roll down your window, and as you are squinting against the harsh light, he cackles, "Heh, heh, getting a little poontang, are ya?" The answer, had it been given, would have been a resounding NO about nine times out of ten. Hardly anyone every got lucky in those days. Those that did, usually ended up having to get married – which started the whole damn ball rolling one more time.

In 1984, my cousin Brian was in Manning and stopped by the Agricultural Hall one night for the wind-up shindig following the Big Rodeo. The hall was like an island in a sea of muck, but inside the mud on the shoes and boots dried in the heat, flaked off and formed millions of particles of dust which became airborne as the dancers twirled and whirled about the crowded room. While standing at the back in the Stag Line, he bumped into Teddy, a bearded, grizzled oldtimer – about thirty-nine years old – who grabbed him in a big bearhug and then invited him outside for a drink. In the trunk of the fellow's car were rows and rows of every kind of liquor imaginable, all lined up in homemade racks. "Name your poison," ordered Teddy, pointing at his portable inventory.

Just then the doors to the hall crashed open and two fellows came hurtling down the steps, propelled by a half-dozen people. Someone yelled, "You know the rules: if you're gonna fight, take it outside." And the two guys hammered away at each other, falling down in the mud, getting up, slipping, staggering, clutching until they spotted Brian and his host, standing there silhouetted against the amber glow emanating from the open trunk of the car. They entered into an instant armistice, linked arms, shuffled over to the inviting array of booze and said, "It's a party —whose buying?" Teddy, rightfully proud of and justifiably proprietary towards his mobile liquor store, said, "Who in hell invited the likes of you."

The two erstwhile pugilists rolled their eyeballs, prodded each other in the ribs with a finger and laughed until they nearly threw up. When they finally recovered and could breathe again properly, one of them said, "Yeah, like we need an invitation to have a drink. Excuuuuuse me, Teddy-boy, we must have been so busy doing the summer fallow we forgot to mail back our RSVP's."

# Bye, George – I Think You Got It
Dwayne W. Rowe

Whenever talk drifts around to the early days of the Battle River Country and to the pioneering spirit of the homesteaders, you can be certain some grizzled oldtimer is going to take a sip on his beverage, suck in a lungful of carcinogenic fog, and start talking about George. The seminal mention of George is enough to stifle all other conversation on fundamental topics like the Constitution, outrageous taxes or who has the biggest hooters at the Roadside Truck Stop and Chapel, Mary-Jo, the cook or Susie Q, the night waitress.

Tippyjar Boomitai, late of Orillia, Ontario, an Orillian visionary known as the Canadian Horace Greely, was reputed to advise people to "Get the hell out of the East," but recent studies by academics have indicated this was not a major factor in westward migration. The dustbowl in Saskatchewan, a worldwide depression and there being not much else to do, were probably a greater motivating influence on those who ended up in that godforsaken Battle River Country, 365 miles north of Edmonton. There is little doubt that those pioneers, despite continuous hardship, deprivation and numbing cold, maintained a vision of a glorious and prosperous future. But, those dreams of neverending fertile fields were often created by rigorous sampling of a unique concoction invented by George.

I am only going to identify George as George. In doing so, I run the risk of people suspecting that this is some kind of a fairy tale. But that is preferable to rampant, wild speculation threatening to point the finger at families of impeccable reputation on the verge of becoming dynasties. The hallmark of a dynasty is that the second generation has deliberately chosen to forget how the original money was made and the third generation just doesn't give a damn. Another problem is that George had become so successful in business by the mid-1950's, acquiring, against all odds, a modicum of respectability, that his customers would read this, dig out their old invoices, and consider legal action over some ancient transaction. The only people who know the truth are members of the Order of The Squirrel, a fraternal drinking society, formed by previous adherents of The Brethren of Old Crow. The Squirrels believed that the purpose of drinking wasn't to get high and hop around, but to go completely nuts. So, having taken the Squirrel Pledge of Secrecy, I am going to tell the story with just a bit of hedging here and there.

About 1929, George came into the Peace Country and, after spending a lifetime in Grimshaw one year, moved on north to the Battle River area. His total worldly possessions consisted of a rickety old Ford, a bedroll, the ragged clothes on his back, a limited command of the English language, lots of German determination and a pretty fair concept of self-esteem. Once he found the whereabouts of his homestead, it didn't take him too long to discover that there was going to be a lot more to the farming business than he had anticipated.

First off, in the scorching July sun, chopping down thirty-foot poplar trees and grubbing out willows made a man thirsty. The alkaline water from the hastily-dug well took away some of the grime at the back of the throat, but didn't make those damn trees any easier to cut. As it is told, and you can take it with a grain of alkaline or not, George stopped the axe in mid-swing, walked back to an old shed back of the small shack that had been built five years before by the previous homesteader, and sat down on a stump. He began poking around inside the shed and found it crammed with odds and ends of hardware, nails, tubing, a clawfooted bathtub full of wheat, pans, buckets and pipe.

The first settler on that piece of ground, an English Remittance Man who couldn't farm or cook, had just up and died one winter from the combined forces of that old double whammy — starvation and despair. The postmaster, after a month or so, decided to bring around the monthly remittance from Old Blighty and found the poor sod sitting up in a chair, stiff, clutching a copy of Burke's Peerage in his hand, fully dressed for dinner, looking quite normal for an English squire, except for being dead.

George surveyed the materials on hand and headed for Notikewin, a wide spot in the road, with a general store and a population of forty souls. About four hours later, Joe the Merchant was laughing himself sick over the way he had stung that dumb Kraut by peddling about three hundred pounds of wet sugar, a couple dozen packages of yeast and his entire stock of stale raisins. The purchases from the hardware section were a bit tough to figure out, but Joe was having too much fun telling his cronies about the scam to give it further thought.

The next day, there was no sound of chopping or falling trees coming from George's homestead. Instead, within a week or so there were delicious noises in the night — hissing, bubbling, boiling and brewing. Local historians concur that the first person to sample George's brew, later renowned under the uncopyrighted brand, Homestead Spirit, was a Dutchman called Rip van Wyck. Rip had dropped by to converse in some kind of hybrid Dutch-German dialect known only to those who lived below sea level and dined on sauerkraut and schnappes. George pressed a cup of murky liquid into Rip's big, lumpy hand, and the two of them began to drink and talk of the Old Country. It was a glorious night — the moon was full and Rip had a chance to get away from his nagging wife, who not only outweighed him by at least thirty pounds, but cussed like a mule-skinner, which is exactly what she had been down in Montana where he met her. Rip, at a mere 220 pounds, was damn well afraid of her and, after the third mug of Homestead Spirit, admitted it. Rip left at dawn and the mules took him home, the sloshing of the liquid in the jug, joining with the sounds of birds singing and Rip's prodigious snoring as he lay in the back of the wagon. In George's pocket, lying there all shiny and cold were two silver dollars.

About noon, the door to George's shack went crashing down as Mrs. Rip filled the doorway, her bulk allowing only a couple of skinny shafts of sunlight, on either side of her enormous neck, to pierce the room.

"You goddamn, hair-brained, no good sonofabitch Kraut wiener," she bellowed, at a volume sufficient to cause the translucent, greased paper stretched over the window frame — an ersatz frontier glass — to vibrate, like a giant kazoo.

"*Vas is los?*" inquired George and found out soon enough as the knotted end of a halter rope slapped up alongside his swollen head.

"My Rip's gone blind, you Bavarian bastard. Blinder'n a bat. The mules brung him home and I found him in the hog trough, lyin' there singing. The man can't see nuthin' 'cept the light of day."

While Wilhemina was cussing him out some more, George jumped out of bed and grabbed for his pants. Mrs. Rip, thinking he might be reaching for a gun, went to head him off. George, who slept naked to save wrinkling his clothes, was about halfway out of the door, pants held in front of private parts, when the damn things — the pants and the private parts — caught on the splintered door jamb.

In the next minute or so until he reached the safety of the poplar bluff, he had been whupped about twenty times with the business end of a wet rope. It is generally agreed that had Wilhemina, The Big Ripper, not run out of breath, she would have killed poor George. Long before the description was applied to Nancy Reagan, Wilhemina was known to be tougher than mule meat.

Rip recovered within a week, although he complained for years about blurry vision and the occasional headache. In terms of causation and resultant trauma, most medical experts I have consulted indicate the lingering symptoms may have been due to repeated and severe blows to the head with a rung from a wooden chair. After Rip regained his ability to distinguish light from dark on a pretty consistent basis, Wilhemina brought George over some supper and an apple pie, explaining that she thought Rip had been blinded for good and that she would have to do all the work, instead of just 90%, the way she had been doing for years. She forgave George and then showed him how to filter out some of the poisons, like fusil oil, rust, bugs, algae and so on. She pitched in to help with the next batch of brew and the colour improved so that it was like an amber sloughwater. The taste was more complex to define and required use of a couple of senses — to put it plainly, it tasted like creosote smells.

Nevertheless each batch seemed to be better than the one before and word spread until the product became a household staple. Distributors were found for each district and the way to George's door became a well trod path. Within a couple of years the clear patch where he had cut down some trees began to reforest itself and the ecosystem was content.

George never bought any more supplies from Joe; instead he arranged to have everything trucked in from Peace River. But not before telling Joe in front of all of the usual hangers-on in the store that sooner, rather than later, he was going to take a baseball bat and pound damp sugar up his ass. Not to leave Joe without an option, George offered the friendly advice that for the next Halloween dance he should go as a candied apple. But it never happened. Joe sold the general store to an outsider that had hitched up to a local girl. By coincidence the closing date of the deal was high noon on October 31. Late that dark and snowy night, a shadowy figure was seen leaving town, dressed in black, wearing a big floppy hat, almost concealing a face that was white as a ghost.

Time went by and with its passage came refinements from the outside world. Edmonton, scary as that seems to us now, was regarded as the cusp of civilization. Increasing prosperity at the end of WWII heralded a change in taste of the average consumer and people started drinking beer and honest-to-Government sealed liquor. George tried to convince his customers that booze was like people — aging just made it weaker — but soon realized that he was left with only a few die-hard clients. For those loyal consumers who stayed on to deplete George's remaining inventory, that is, in fact, exactly how they died.

The hallmark of the true entrepreneur is the ability to adapt to a new world order and George made the switch from manufacturer and wholesaler to retail distributor. The nearest place to buy "hard liquor" was at the "Government Drugstore" in Peace River, about seventy miles from Manning, the new town created for the sole purpose of selling beer. As an afterthought, it was named to honour Premier Ernest C. Manning of "Back To The Bible Hour" radio fame, who never had a drink in his life. The Mackenzie Highway was pretty awful most of the time, which may account for the fact that Sir Alexander travelled mainly by canoe. It took a special type of vehicle and George's new Buick was well suited for carrying a bit of extra weight, such as cases of whiskey. On one occasion, George left for Peace River on a Friday afternoon to pick up enough stuff to handle the crowd at the annual Harvest Dance. About halfway home, he ran into a wicked downpour that turned the gumbo into glue at the bottom of a small hill and the overloaded Buick soon bogged down to the axles. After an hour or so, mired in the middle of the roadway, the rain stopped. A couple of hours later the sun came through the mist and so did Corporal McDonald of the RCMP in his cheap, light-weight and sparsely provisioned government car. Riding up on top of the goop, the good Corporal made it across the worst part of the muck to the high ground. He pulled over and walked back to the stranded Buick. Dressed in his finest, having served all week as Court Officer for the Supreme Court Assizes at Peace River, McDonald leaned against the large Buick, drummed his fingers on the roof and started to chuckle.

"Well, George," said the Corporal. "On your way to go dancing?"

"I kinda figgered on it," said George. "If it's dry there."

"I'm sure that's why you're headed there, Mister! Let's look inside your car."

It didn't take more than a glance to discover the entire back seat was loaded with cases of booze, covered over by an old Hudson's Bay blanket and a sleeping bag.

"Move your car over towards mine," snapped the Corporal. "And load this booze into it, easy-like, and don't drop any."

George started the car and slowly let out the clutch, riding it, gently feeding the accelerator until the rear tires were slipping on the mud. He carefully fed it a bit more gas, swinging the steering wheel back and forth until it spun sideways, bucking and rearing, before settling down into the ruts.

"Damn it," muttered McDonald. "Goose the damn thing and I'll push."

As the skookum, red tunic-clad Maintainer-of-All-That-Is-Right bent to the frame of the Buick, George let out the clutch, tromped on the accelerator and roared off, leaving McDonald prone, headfirst in the slop. The good Corporal leapt to his feet, mud-spattered, red-faced, the Irish in him roiling out of his massive body and he yelled, "You sonofabitch, I'll get you if its the last bloody thing I ever do."

Corporal McDonald was able to commiserate with another police officer, a Constable Sturn who was doing four weeks duty around the Manning area, filling in for the regular who went away for a while to some kind of treatment centre for Mounties. Soon after reporting for duty, Constable Sturn had stopped George at a roadblock, after having received a visit from an outraged Pentecostal choir lady claiming someone was doing the Devil's Work. She explained she had watched George for about two hours, laboriously loading boxes into the back of his car. She described in some detail the clinking and rattling of bottles. Sturn, after searching the Buick and finding several cardboard boxes, ripped open the flaps to reveal jars of canned dill pickles, peaches and chokecherries. Like a damn fool, he asked George what happened to the liquor.

"I sold it," said George. "Constable, do I look like a drinking man. That's my business, buyin' and sellin'. People want hay, I sell them hay. They want booze I sell them..."

"I know, " said Sturn. "But how in hell do you keep getting away with it?"

"That, Constable," said George, "is why I'm still in business."

And, with that he drove away, reflecting that the next time some busybody dropped by the detachment office for a cup of tea and a little gossip, The Horsemen might not be so quick to respond. He also made a mental note to drop by the Alliance Tabernacle and drop a fifty dollar bill in the Missionary Relief Fund in aid of the Lord's work.

From the mid-thirties until the end of the war, for some reason, the sale of beaver pelts was illegal in Alberta. It had something to do with a perceived shortage of the toothsome critter due, perhaps, to an epidemic of Beaver Fever. Whatever the cause, the national symbol was becoming scarce. Albertans were prohibited from dealing in that sought-after fur, which was bringing about $40 a skin in British Columbia and other parts of Canada, especially back east in Montreal where the big furriers were located. Native Indians were permitted to trap beaver but couldn't sell them or trade for needed supplies. Then, to make things worse, along came a ban on muskrat.

George, much like Mother Nature herself, abhorred a vacuum and again saw the need for an honest broker to straighten out the economy. The Mounties, ever on guard to illegal trafficking in the national mammal, once more restored George's name to the top of their shitlist. The problem was that there were people who were eager to buy the beaver pelts — a ready market existed and the markup beat the hell out of that charged on flour and salt. For those wanting to deal in the pelts, it was a dangerous game as the Mounties, now with a detachment of more than a dozen, and with newer cars, would stop any vehicle suspected of hauling furs. When nabbed, stiff jail sentences were handed out to offenders by a cooperative judiciary, even to first-time offenders. Several arrests and convictions resulted, but none of the pelt-runners had any connections whatsoever with George.

A good piece of advice for people dealing with Mounties is — don't be fooled by the Musical Ride — they are a persistent bunch and harboured the knowledge, deep inside their guts, that George was somehow, somewhere doing something illegal. It's a visceral thing with them, hard to explain, like a Socialist always suspecting that somebody is making some money and maybe keeping a bit of it for himself. However, suspicious though they were, there was no proof of any wrongdoing on George's part.

In fact there was evidence to the contrary. George became involved in politics, acting as chauffeur and guide to the MLA who was seeking re-election. George took him up to Fort Vermillion, where mainstreeting and canvassing the entire town were the same thing, introducing him to several native leaders and local voters. He even went so far as to pay for the hotel room overnight. In the morning, after George and the MLA finished a congenial breakfast with the local Mountie, George volunteered to pack the politician's suitcase and carry it out to the car. Next day, back at the

MLA's home, George hauled the bag inside the house and then asked the fellow, somewhat plaintively, "Is it okay with you if I take my beaver back now?" George snapped the case open to reveal the furry contents and the People's Chosen Representative grabbed at his chest and sat down hard on the sofa. "Don't you . . . " he spluttered, "ever do that to me again."

"Okay," said George. "You got yourself a deal. I just realized I'm not cut out for politics anyway."

"Where in hell are my clothes," the MLA inquired.

"Traded the suit and those fancy white shirts for the beaver," said George. "Give me your measurements and I'll send you some new stuff."

George, always an avuncular fellow, began to spend a considerable amount of time with a local native family. One of the daughters, Nancy, had a husband who was up in Keg River working a trapline. She was rumoured to be having a difficult pregnancy which required the kind of sophisticated medical attention available only from a silver-haired smoothie physician practicing in Peace River.

A couple of times a month, George would drive her, accompanied by her mother, to see the doctor and to get prescriptions filled at the pharmacy. The Mounties became accustomed to seeing George, in the company of the pretty, but increasingly round, young lady and her omnipresent mother. After a visit to the doctor the threesome wandered in and out of various stores and shops in town. In fact, the mounties became convinced that George had turned the corner and was atoning for past sins. It wasn't unusual for one or more of the Mounties to stop the trio on the sidewalk and to speculate about the gender of the soon-to-arrive infant and joke about the probability the baby would be named either George or Georgina, in honour or the young mother's patron. Nancy would waddle into a drygoods store or butcher shop and a few minutes later would come out with a new hat or coat and was always carrying some large parcel, proudly held in front of her for all to see. She and her mom would pile into George's new Buick and away they would go, across the bridge over the Mighty Peace, up the hill and on north to Manning.

Several months passed and one day a couple of Mounties, sitting in their patrol car eating a bag of doughnuts, happened to see Nancy, huge by this time, slowly make her way into a store. One of the Mounties was pretending to have binoculars by looking through a couple of doughnut holes when he noticed Nancy come out of the doorway. He dropped the doughnuts and, being the trained observer he was, examined her with his naked eye, unaided by any technological optical device. Nancy —was skinny as a rail! They were convinced she had delivered a baby inside the store and ran in to see if they could assist in some way or other as Nancy was clearly in a daze. A quick search of the premises revealed there was no baby and they ran back outside, catching up with Nancy, who spoke only Cree to police officers and missionaries. One constable, Big Jake, made a hoop of his arms, extending them out in front of his belly, and made "Waa, Waa, Waa" noises. The other policeman, Handsome Dan, pointed at Nancy's trim abdomen and went "Goo-Goo, Gaa-Gaa." Nancy shrugged in that wonderfully polite but completely detached way the Cree have when confronted by nincompoops. She ran across the street to George's car, jumped in, and fluttered those elegant fingers in a farewell wave as George tromped the gas and disappeared in the dust.

Back at the detachment, the boys started comparing notes and soon realized that Nancy had been pregnant for at least a year. One of the young Mounties wondered aloud if the Doctor's wife's new fur coat didn't have just a smidgen of a homemade look about it. When pressed for details by the other officers, he muttered something about the back hem being out of whack and let the subject drop. The next morning a package arrived at the barracks addressed to: The Commanding Officer And All the King's Men. The Mounties assembled in the coffee room and opened the parcel to find a dozen packs of White Owl cigars neatly laid out in rows with a card lying on top that read, "Fine boy born yesterday morning. Weighed five beaver pelts and a muskrat hide. He shall be called Little Beaver." And the card was signed, "Uncle George."

The Inspector, a fine French-Canadian fellow, said, "Dat bugger, dat is one smart bugger." And the boys said to hell with it, went to the Exhibits Locker, took out a bottle of Homestead Spirit they had seized off a drunk in an alley, and smoked the White Owls, pretty well killing off the entire day.

By the early fifties, George was still buying and selling all kinds of things but he did so from properly licensed retail outlets. George had pretty much stopped selling liquor but still kept the odd case or two on hand for special occasions when people needed some cheer. By now, the detachment at Peace River had become so sophisticated that they had plainclothes officers who would sneak up and down the highway, dressed as peddlers or big-city types out for a look at the Peace Country. George ran a small garage with two gas pumps and a cafe and the precise password used by folks looking to buy a jug was "I'd like some gas line antifreeze." One November day, a couple of smartly dressed fellows came into the garage and, pausing for a moment in their salesman-type banter, asked George if he had a little something that they could put in their tank — like, maybe some special stuff that wouldn't freeze. George told them, no problem, and went into the back of the garage, returning with a whiskey bottle, stopped-up with a cork, telling them that it would cost them each five dollars. The cops handed over the money, and one of them pulled out the cork and said, "By Geesus, we got you now." He put the jug to his mouth took a big gulp (solely for the purpose of being able to swear later in Court that the liquid was really liquor), and then collapsed on the floor, coughing, hacking, retching and spewing the contents of his burning mouth onto the sawdust-covered linoleum.

"Shit, Bill," he croaked to his befuddled partner, "The

goddamn gasoline is . . . gasoline."

"Sure thing," said George, "most people around here use it to run their cars. Only guy I knew drank it was old Goofy Fogarty and he was crazier'n a coot."

The two dicks left the place, forgetting to reclaim their two five-dollar bills, which they found out they needed when they went to pay for a meal at the Chinese cafe and came up short for the Chop Suey. Fong, whom they were always trying to bust for running Mah Jongg games, made them put up both of their watches for security and they went back to talk to George who was more than willing to issue a refund. He opened the till and asked them to help themselves. The two dicks were looking for their two marked bills, each with an "X" on the upper right-hand corner. They found them right away and then decided to examine the other thirty or forty five-dollar bills in the tray. All of them had a pencilled-in cross on the upper right-hand corner. George told them it wasn't fitting or proper for the Queen's Representatives to be carrying around defaced currency and gave them a couple of fresh, crisp ones out of his new billfold.

The detectives drove off but before heading back to Peace River stopped by the shack occupied by their usually reliable, albeit stupid, informant. A couple of days later this guy, known to townspeople by his nickname, Snitch, was seen hobbling around town with a sore rear-end, which he tried to pass off as a bad case of piles.

George's boys followed his teaching and branched out into various businesses. They did well enough to buy an airplane. They took their pilot's training and became fully licensed, authorized and insured aircraft owners and operators. One summer day, a fellow hopped out of a plain, brown Chevrolet and came into the coffee shop. There he saw George, all dressed up, fresh from a funeral, wearing his ball cap and jacket, aviator sunglasses, sitting in a booth sipping his coffee. George invited the stranger to join him, chatted with the fellow for a few minutes and then asked if he was in town to do some goose hunting. The man said he'd like to do that but had some work to do. It turned out he was an auditor for the Department of National Revenue, a precursor of Revenue Canada (the old Tax Department got cursed at just like the new Rev Can) and he confided that he was looking for a certain man called George So and So.

"I know that guy," said George. "I think he's a crook, probably hiding money out at his place across the river a few miles from here. Never liked the man. Hell, you can't even get there by car. I'll fly you there in my plane. I got a hunting lodge just over the hill where he usually hides out."

They went to the little airstrip a hundred yards out back of the garage and climbed into a Cessna 172. George cranked over the engine and without too much in the way of a pre-flight check, except checking the runway, up and down, for cows, took off straight downwind. It wasn't as though George had any aversion to chopping critters into halves, quarters, or grinding them up for hamburger — he had been doing that most of his life — rather, he'd grown accustomed to using high-quality German tools, instead of propellers, and he preferred the animals to be mostly dead before he started any cutting. The Cessna lifted off, a bit wobbly at first but it soon gained altitude and headed out over the hills like a big-assed bird. George put the aircraft into a steep bank now and then and told his passenger to keep looking out the window straight at the ground, especially during the tight turns. He flew low over some trees, skimmed along the river, zoomed up over some cutbanks and followed a cutline, straight as an arrow sticking into the heart of the bush. He weaved and bobbed, climbing up into the clouds and then scooted down low, just over the fence lines. He saw a couple of moose just about to copulate and gave them a cold-air shower from the prop wash. His passenger had been fairly chatty for the first ten or fifteen minutes but had become extremely quiet.

"Don't see that sonofabitch, George, that you're lookin'

for," said George. "Might as well head back."

A few minutes of straight and level flight brought some colour back into the civil servant's pasty cheeks and he began to make conversation over the roar of the engine.

"How many hours you got in?" he asked George.

"Bout three-quarters," George replied.

"No," yelled the guy. "I mean how many hours of flying time you got."

"A-BOUT FOR-TEE FIVE MIN-UTES," George hollered into his ear and then went on to explain that one of these days he was going to bite the bullet and take some flying lessons, what with the provincial government giving out a rebate on the price of training for new pilots.

"You mean you ... you ... don't have a license," stammered the bewildered taxman.

"Won't give me one," said George. "Not until they change that rule about needing more than one good eye."

George had put in hundreds of hours riding in the right-hand seat, watching his boys handle that plane, and the Cessna is pretty forgiving in any event. He came around on final approach, throttled her back so that the prop was just ticking over sweet and regular and the plane was sinking down gently, like a fat kid in a haystack. Just before touchdown, a nasty little crosswind gusted up from across the highway but George crabbed the gutsy little Cessna into the wind and had it pretty well straightened out before the tires bit the dirt on that little strip. George was used to the Buick and reacted a bit too heavily on the throttle but still managed to perform what is known in the business as a perfect 15-point landing.

For those not familiar with aviation terms, that is defined in all the manuals as a 3-point landing done very quickly, five times in a row. In tournament competition, in order to extract a perfect 6.0 score from the judges — who tend to be picky, crabby old bastards — it is necessary to fully compress the landing apparatus to the maximum each time any part of the tricycle landing gear comes into rude and abrupt contact with the surly bonds of earth. On this occassion, the only person holding up any cardboard was a hitchiker on the side of the road with a destination sign and he would have awarded 6.5 out of 6.0, after factoring in the degree of difficulty. The plane covered a lot of the runway, including some side to side travel, and came to a stop in a small pile of straw at the end of the field, the prop chewing up the stuff into a yellowy powder. When the auditor came to, revived by a slug of something from a flask, he walked across the field back to the garage, moving funny-like with his legs held real close together. He headed straight for the men's toilet where he stayed for a long, long time. When he came out, George was gone and nobody in the coffee shop let on they knew what in hell he was babbling about. The guy just jumped in his car and left town.

A few months later, George's accountant phoned to say that the Department had decided not to do any reassessments or revised income statements as it was common knowledge, even in Edmonton, that the Manning country had suffered another poor crop year and even the merchants were going broke. George wanted the accountant to write to the auditor asking if he did end up taking some flying lessons, would they be deductible. The accountant, one of those guys that just didn't quite have the personality to make it as an actuary, advised him not to kick a sleeping dog in the ass and sent a bill based on that professional judgment which George paid by return mail.

Well, there isn't a lot left to tell. Pavement and cable TV came to the Manning country. The town has a swimming pool, a library and there is even a video rental place. Just before the pavement went in, there was a flood which was backing up water onto George's business premises. He wasn't getting any satisfaction from the local MLA, who was still pissed off about the beaver-in-the-suitcase incident, so he jumped on a D-8 Cat and cut a hole in the road. The resident engineer in Peace River, a dead ringer for Billy Barty, nearly had a conniption fit. He jumped up on a stool and phoned his boss, Gordon Taylor, the Minister of Highways, who promptly left for the weekend to visit his constituents in Drumheller, where the land is so bad and deep-down ugly, it's become a tourist attraction. Meanwhile back in Manning, the water drained away and a few days later George jumped back on the Cat, filled the hole with gravel from the government stockpile and life went on. The mud dried up and the wind blew and the dust flew as the big eighteen-wheelers rolled up and down the highway.

There is no question that genetics are the truest thing on earth. Any stockbreeder or horseracing expert will vouch for that. Not so long ago, one of George's boys sold a house trailer, on credit, to a fellow who had the misfortune to skip a few payments. One snowy, blowy, forty-below night, George's boy and a drinking buddy jumped into a one-ton truck, drove over to the trailer park at 3:00 AM, knocked out the props holding up the trailer and hitched it up to the truck. It's not as though they hadn't tried to get legal advice but their snotty lawyer in Peace River just screamed obscenities at them and slapped the phone down real hard. Inside the trailer, now being towed down the highway at about fifty miles an hour, was the sleeping debtor, unaware that he was in the process of changing his postal code. Lying in his bunk, being rocked to and fro by the passage of his residence — which was literally goin' down the road — the man was oblivious to the inescapable application of the universal adage — if you don't pay your exorcist or your trailer payments, then one fateful night you will get re-possessed. The trailer hit a bump on the highway where some snow had drifted and frozen solid, and the chap inside the trailer fell out of bed. He picked himself up and peered out the window. He saw darkness, blowing snow, ice crystals and trees, which was exactly the view he was used to, looking out at his back yard.

What he couldn't make any sense of was the two guys on Ski Doos chasing a coyote along a ditch. He pulled on a pair of slippers and some pants, threw on a parka and stepped outside to see what was going on. Since he was up and out anyway, he planned on taking a quick pee, in preparation for which, he took matters in hand. He hit the ground at about 40 mph, running and voiding a mighty stream, legs churning like free-wheeling pistons, arms waving a hundred fast goodbyes to the rear end of his trailer, now disappearing around a curve. He somersaulted to a stop, curled up inside his parka like a Danish roll-mop, and lay there for a while, buried inside a snowbank. A few minutes later, he backed out of the snowhole, got cleaned off and waited in the cold until a passing stranger in a pickup saw him standing on the side of the road and gave him a lift into town. He went straightaway to the Mounties and reported that his house was missing. The rookie cop couldn't find the Missing House Report Form and had to make do with making a note on some scrap paper. The Mountie drove the fellow back to the highway but all they could see was a big "angel" in the snow, as if made by the biggest, dumbest kid ever to go to a daycare. They followed the trail back from the angel to the centre of the highway — where all they found was a fifteen-foot-long thin, yellow icicle.

The denouement —which is French for bottom line — was the guy scraped off some skin but also scraped up the missing payments and the trailer went back to its rightful position, perched proudly on some forty-five-gallon oil drums. George's boy waived any interest accruing on the arrears and they had a couple of drinks and told hunting stories until the early hours. Troubles, like any wound, tend to scab over after a while and provided you don't pick away at them, are soon forgotten.

George died a few years ago, his final days made more comfortable knowing the federal government had followed Alberta's lead and abolished all inheritance taxes. For a while, it looked as though George would either have to take his money with him or hide it in the old icehouse, under the sawdust, the way he had done with the beaver pelts. The icehouse was in a pretty sorry state but could have been restored in a way that made it impervious to the high-tech infra-red scanners used by modern-day revenooers to seek out hot, hidden money. George's dwindling time was spun out playing cards with his cronies, sipping a bit of good whiskey, and reflecting on the half-century he had spent married to his wife, the hardest working woman God had ever created and the best business partner in the universe.

George's boys and their children have become very successful in business following the old rules that have now hardened into tradition — sell a good product in an area of little or no competition, to hell with any after-sale service, and keep minimal records.

So, if what I've told you here isn't the whole truth and nothing but the truth, then I rest my defence on the credo of the Order of the Squirrel. Times change, but people don't. There will always be folks drinking booze, telling lies, and some guy, somewhere, will find himself trapped in a slough of deep, deep despond for having succumbed to the allure of illicit and forbidden beaver.

## Hal C. Sisson

was born in Moose Jaw, Saskatchewan. He was a reporter for the Saskatchewan Star-Phoenix, then a lawyer for 30 years in Alberta. He retired in 1984 to devote time to croquet, marble collecting and writing fiction. He and Dwayne Rowe founded the Peace Players, whose annual burlesque show enjoyed a 25-year run. Sisson is the author of *The Big Bamboozle* and *Caverns of the Cross*. His goal is "to write more fiction before bucket-kicking time." He lives in Victoria, BC.

## Dwayne W. Rowe

hails from Northern Alberta, "So far up the map it made your nose bleed." He practised law with Hal Sisson in Peace River, Alberta from 1963 to 1969, and has defended clients or served as a judge in about 150 Canadian communities, from St. John's to Old Crow. He has written comedy for CBC radio and television and sold jokes to Joan Rivers. Rowe is a deputy judge of the Tax Court of Canada and lives in the seaside community of Sidney, BC.